the Rookie

S R SILCOX

THE ROOKIE

Copyright © S R Silcox, 2025

First published 2025

Published by Juggernaut Books PL

Email: mail@srsilcox.com

URL: https://www.srsilcox.com

This is a work of fiction. Name, characters, places and incidents are a product of the author's imagination. Any resemblance to actual persons, events or locales is entirely coincidental.

The Rookie

Silcox, S R

First Edition

Paperback ISBN 978-0-6458503-4-5

For Sonia Hughes. Who never got to show what she was capable of.

AUTHOR NOTE

I AM AN AUSSIE sapphic author, and this book is set in Australia. So if my words seem to be incorrectly spelled, please note that they are not. I write in Australia's version of English.

Quick note for the purists: I know most of the world calls it 'football', but depending on where you live, that could mean rugby, gridiron, Aussie rules... you get the idea. The only game that ever gets called 'soccer' is, well, soccer. So forgive me for using the 's-word' for the beautiful game throughout this book.

(I promise I call it football at home).

SR

x

ONE

Saving a four-year-old's life wasn't on Lindsay McAllister's To Do list that Monday morning, but she was glad she was in the right place at the right time.

She'd been spreading woodchip in the junior playground when a soccer ball careened out of nowhere and headed straight for a toddler playing on a spring-loaded rocker. Without thinking, Lindsay took a stride to her right, stretched out her hand, and parried the ball away, saving the toddler from certain death, or what would have felt like it to the poor kid if the ball had hit him. His mother ran over, horrified and thankful, checking on her son who was still rocking back and forth on the spring rocker, oblivious to the danger he'd been in only moments before.

For Lindsay, it was instinct. Years of honing her skills in the goal box of the semi-professional clubs she'd played for meant she'd made the save without thinking. After ensuring both the toddler and his mum were okay, Lindsay turned to where the ball had come from. A teenage boy was ambling over. Lindsay held up the ball. "Yours?"

The boy nodded. Lindsay over-armed the ball back and turned back to her work.

"You've still got it," a voice said behind her.

Lindsay spun around to see where the voice had come from.

"The stride, the reach. I'd know that form any-where."

Lindsay grinned. "Den."

"You still jump like a gazelle," Den teased, pulling Lindsay in for a hug and then releasing her to hold her at arm's length. "Some reflexes."

"They still work fine when I've got gloves on," Lindsay shot back, wiggling her hands in her work gloves. She narrowed her eyes. "Wait. How did you even know where to find me?"

"Pop told me," Den said with a shrug.

Lindsay rolled her eyes. "Of course he did." She'd be talking to him when she got home tonight.

Den gave Lindsay a friendly shove. "It's been way too long since our last catch up."

"You're the one flitting all over the place," Lindsay said. "Me? I'm not going anywhere. I'm easy to find."

Den raised an eyebrow. "Easy to find, sure. But stuck in one place? That's not living, Linds. That's just… existing."

Lindsay shrugged, hiding behind a smile. "Nothing wrong with being settled."

Den smirked. "You always did like pretending standing still was a choice. Meanwhile, I'm still chasing the game."

Lindsay rolled her eyes. "Is that why you're here?"

"It is, actually. We've got our final on Saturday. I wanted to do a reccy on the stadium."

"You're not still playing?" Lindsay wasn't surprised. Out of all the players she'd played with, Denise Baker was the most likely to still be playing in her forties.

"Coaching," Den replied. "Oakridge Mustangs."

"You never mentioned that. When did that happen?" Lindsay smiled despite herself. That certainly didn't surprise her either. Den ate, slept and breathed soccer. So did Lindsay, once.

"I've been in the job a couple of months. Still finding my feet."

"Pop did mention a game this weekend but I thought it was just locals."

"That's ours," Den confirmed. "Grand final. And if we win, we'll be playing in the new Champions League Tournament."

Pop had mentioned something about that too. New world-cup-style professional club tournament for the best clubs from around Australia. It was impressive that Den was coaching at that level.

"Are you coming to watch?" Den asked.

Lindsay turned away. "Nope."

"Let me rephrase that," Den said. "I'd like you to come and have a look at a 'keeper of mine. She's got something special but there's a block I can't work out. I want to renew her contract but I'm under pressure to let her go."

"I don't do soccer anymore, Den, you know that," Lindsay replied with a shrug.

"That save back there says otherwise," Den said, teasing.

Lindsay ignored her. Working outdoors had kept her fit, and the ball wasn't that far away, so she would've been disappointed if she'd missed it.

"Just take a look at her," Den said. "She's really something special."

"They all are," Lindsay said. How many times had she heard that exact same thing said about herself? It was a meaningless thing to say. She picked up the shovel and pushed it into the wood-chip on the trailer and dumped a pile into the wheelbarrow.

"Ellie's just got that certain something," Den said. "Like you did."

Lindsay scoffed.

"No, really, Linds. She does. But there's something stopping her from reaching her potential and I could really do with your advice."

Lindsay turned away. Den persisted.

"Come to training on Friday. Watch her. Tell me what you think."

"I'm busy on Friday," Lindsay said.

"I thought you might say that," Den said with a chuckle. "Here."

She held out a DVD in a clear case.

"A DVD?" Lindsay joked. "You're still living in the 90s."

Den smiled. "I know what you're like with emails."

Lindsay couldn't argue with that. She only had social media because it was a necessary evil for her business. She took the DVD. She figured Den would go away if she took it, but she had no intention of watching it.

Den checked her watch. "I have to get to the grounds, but let me know what you think." She turned and walked away.

"I can't promise I'll watch it," Lindsay called after her.

"Then don't," Den said. "But she could be better than you."

Lindsay pulled a face at Den's back. No-one could be better than Lindsay was at her best. It wasn't something Lindsay was egotistical about. She was great back then. A potential superstar before women could even be such a thing. But she never got to reach her potential on the field. She'd made her peace with it and had moved on.

Lindsay dropped the DVD into her lunchbox. There was no way she was watching it, and no way in hell was she having anything to do with professional soccer again.

She spread the last of the woodchip, picked up the wheelbarrow and pushed it back to the trailer. As she pulled more woodchip into the wheelbarrow, her phone buzzed. She pulled it out of her pocket and jammed it between her ear and shoulder.

"Mac's Maintenance," she answered, leaning the shovel against the side of the trailer.

"Sorry I haven't been answering," her contractor, Rod, said.

"I know you're not busy," Lindsay half-joked. "What's happening?"

"I'm trying to get your pay together," Rod said. "I'm sorry it's late, it's just the company's being a pain in my arse."

"Third time," Lindsay said, taking the phone with her hand and leaning on the back of her ute. "I can't live on air, Rod."

"I know, mate. Believe me, I know." There was silence on the other end of the phone. Lindsay could picture Rod in his office, raking his hands over his face. "Look, I can transfer some money this afternoon for you, a part-payment, just until I can sort out what's happening with head office. I can probably get the rest by the end of next week."

Lindsay pinched the bridge of her nose. Something was better than nothing. "Yep, fine." She could hear Rod's relieved sigh on the other end of the phone.

"Thanks, Linds."

"You can thank me by paying your bills," Lindsay said, and hung up. She pocketed her phone and picked up the shovel. It was days like today that she really wondered why she decided to start her own business. Chasing up creditors was not what she wanted to spend her time on, especially when they were mates. But at least she got to work outside, doing something physical.

She glanced toward the clearing where the boy from earlier was playing park soccer with his mates. He was showing off, making easy saves into spectacular ones. Flashy meant inefficient. His feet weren't set for a shot and any decent striker would put one past him before he could even blink.

For a moment, Lindsay imagined her work gloves were keeping gloves, tight and dependable. She squeezed the handle of the shovel, imagining the thud of the ball against her palms. Thoughts for what could have been knocked at her brain, but she quickly shut them out and went back to shovelling woodchip.

TWO

On Wednesday afternoon, Lindsay's phone pinged with a text as she drove into her driveway. *Transferred another $500. Will send the rest next week.*

Something was better than nothing, sure, but her contractor owed her a lot more than five hundred dollars. If he didn't pay her in the next week or two, she'd have to take on some smaller cash jobs to tide her over. The whole point of taking the contract with Rod was so she could simplify her business and not have to run around trying to make ends meet with a million and one small jobs.

She took the front steps two at a time and leaned on the door frame to pull her work boots off. She placed them on the shoe rack beside the door and padded up the hallway in her socks.

The TV was blaring from the lounge room. She stuck her head in on her way past.

"I'm home," she called to the back of her Pop's head.

He turned and looked over the top of his recliner. "There's lasagne in the oven."

Lindsay smiled. Even before he retired, Pop liked to cook. Gran baked, Pop cooked, and Lindsay and her friends ate. That was the unspoken deal when she came to live with them. Food was her grandparents' love language, and Lindsay had had to work harder than most of her teammates to stay fit, back when she was chasing stupid childhood dreams.

Although the baking had all but stopped - Pop could make pikelets and Anzac biscuits, but anything else was a bit of a stretch - the cooking had not. Lasagna was a favourite because Lindsay got to take the leftovers to work the next day.

"I'll have a shower first," Lindsay called as she dropped her lunch box and water bottle in the kitchen. She pulled the oven door open and breathed in, closing her eyes.

Cheesy, meaty, saucy perfection. Exactly the way he'd always made it. Exactly the way Lindsay liked it. She took a spoon from the cutlery drawer, dug a corner of the lasagne from the tray, blew on it, and shoved it into her mouth. Just as she was about to dig out another spoonful, Pop called, "Don't eat it off the tray."

Lindsay smiled and closed the oven. "I'm not," she called out of the side of her mouth. She placed the spoon in the sink and headed back down the hallway. "Want to watch a movie after dinner?"

Pop's arm extended above the back of the lounge. Thumbs up. No way he was missing The Price is Right finale though. Lindsay stepped into the room, kissed him on his balding head and then headed back out to the bathroom.

By the time Lindsay had showered and tossed her work clothes into the laundry, Pop had dished up the lasagne, added some salad and had set up two kitchen chairs in the lounge room to use as tables. He was just sitting back in his seat when Lindsay sat down on the recliner next to her Pop's. She opened a beer and handed it to him. He took the bottle and pointed the remote at the TV with his other hand.

"What are we watching?" Lindsay asked, as she sliced off a piece of lasagne and stuck it in her mouth.

"The one you brought home," Pop replied.

"I didn't bring one home," Lindsay said, confused.

"The DVD that was in your lunch box," Pop said.

"I can empty my own lunch box," Lindsay replied. She should have tossed that DVD out.

Pop side-eyed her.

Lindsay rolled her eyes. "Just because I don't empty it straight away doesn't mean I won't get to it."

It was the same argument they'd been having for years, and one that Lindsay was yet to win. Before Lindsay could grab the remote, a training session appeared on the screen. The sound was muted, but Lindsay could see it was a goalkeeping session. Lindsay reached across her Pop for the remote but he pulled it away.

"What's this?" he asked.

"No idea," Lindsay replied.

Pop leaned forward in his chair, taking a bite of his dinner without moving his eyes away from the screen. "Who is it?"

"Just some 'keeper Den wanted help with," Lindsay replied.

The mention of Den got Pop's attention. "Denise Baker?"

"Yes, Denise Baker," Lindsay replied. "She came to see me at work on Monday, but you already know that."

Pop didn't acknowledge the accusation. Instead he said, "She said she wanted to have the team settled before the game."

"You knew she was coming?" Lindsay asked. Why was she the last to know about everything?

"She's coaching the Mustangs. I did tell you about it," Pop said.

"Allegedly," Lindsay muttered. Despite her reluctance otherwise, she couldn't help but watch the goalkeeper on the screen. She was young, that much was obvious. Not overly tall for a keeper from what Lindsay could tell from the video, but she had fast feet and good hands.

"They're training on Friday. Open session," Pop said. "I thought I'd take the kids along. They'll love seeing a proper professional session."

"You never told me that," Lindsay said, looking directly at her Pop.

He shrugged. "It's in the afternoon. I'll be fine."

"I can drop you off and pick you up," Lindsay said.

"I said I'll be fine." Pop rarely got angry or annoyed, but say one thing about his driving and you were toast.

"Tell that to Mrs Henderson's wheelie bin," Lindsay countered, keeping her tone light.

Pop shook his head. "She should have put it away like everyone else in the street. It's an eyesore, you know, leaving it out on the street like that. I've got a right mind to write to the council again."

Lindsay snorted. The council doing something about Mrs Henderson leaving her wheelie bins out was about as likely as Lindsay helping Den. And that was less than zero.

On the screen, the goalkeeper made a fingertip save high in a top corner. Lindsay and Pop both sucked in a breath. "Impressive," Pop said. "What did Denise want?"

"She wanted me to help with her goalkeeper. This one, I guess. I told her no, before you ask."

Pop loaded up his fork with lasagne and salad. "Doesn't look like anything's wrong to me."

"Her weight distribution's wrong," Lindsay said through a mouthful of lasagne.

Pop looked sideways at her.

"What?" Lindsay shrugged.

Pop arched an eyebrow. "I thought you weren't interested."

"I'm not. Can we watch something else now?"

Pop ignored her and pointed the remote at the TV and fast-forwarded the video until he found what he was looking for.

"Game drills," he said.

Lindsay let out a breath, but it was useless arguing with him. He was a coach from way back, and if Den said there was something going on with her 'keeper, then Pop was determined to find out. Not that a video of a training session would prove anything. As if reading her mind, he said, "We need to watch her under pressure."

"We do not," Lindsay replied.

Pop glanced at Lindsay. "You're dropping me off, so you may as well stay."

Lindsay eyeballed him and took a long drink of her beer. Pop smirked and looked back to the TV. "She trains better than you."

Lindsay snorted. "Anyone could train better than me." Could this keeper play better than Lindsay, though? Unlikely, Lindsay thought. Was Lindsay going to spend her Friday afternoon at a training session to find out? Absolutely not.

THREE

ON FRIDAY AFTERNOON, WHILE Pop and his under nines were watching the Mustangs training session, Lindsay sat in the car making phone calls, chasing up Rod for the money he owed, and invoicing for the smaller jobs she'd had to take on to make ends meet.

By the time Pop opened the passenger door and hopped in, Lindsay had calculated that she was working for next to nothing while her contractor wasn't paying his invoices.

"Parmis?" Pop asked, sliding into the seat and pulling on his seat belt.

"Do you want to go home first?" Lindsay asked as she pulled out of the car park.

Pop shook his head. "Nope. Let's beat the rush."

Lindsay nodded and instead of turning left for home, she turned right for the Tavern.

Parmis at the Tavern was their end of week ritual, something they'd done for years, no matter what else was going on. Pop swore it served the best parmagianas in Queensland. Lindsay didn't mind the habit. She liked not having to cook, but tonight she'd have rather gone home. Her mind wasn't on pub food, not with Rod still ghosting her calls and texts.

The pub was packed when they arrived, but Pop weaved his way to their usual table, always kept open by the owner, Craig, a former player from Pop's earlier days as a coach. Lindsay made sure Pop was settled before heading over to the bar to order their dinner and drinks.

"Usual?" Craig asked.

"It's like there's nothing else on the menu," Lindsay joked.

"One parmy, no salad, load up the chips, and a steak and salad, medium," Craig said, tapping on the screen. Lindsay glanced back over at Pop, who was chatting to some people at the table next to him. She smiled to herself. He was such a social butterfly, and everyone loved him. She should be so lucky to inherit just a smidgen of his goodness.

Without asking her drink order, Craig poured Pop's pot of beer and added a dash of Sarsparilla. He popped the top off a glass bottle of coke for Lindsay and poured it into a glass full of ice. As Lindsay paid, a voice beside her said, "You must be Lindsay."

Lindsay turned. A woman she didn't recognise stood there, smiling like they'd known each other for years. About as tall as Lindsay, neat blonde ponytail, Mustangs polo shirt with 'MT' under the logo.

"Den sent me over," the woman said, offering her hand. "Meg. I'm the operations manager for the Mustangs."

Lindsay shook her hand. Something about the easy confidence in Meg's smile tugged at her. "Ops manager, huh?"

"I'm the brains of the operation," Meg said. She glanced over her shoulder. "Don't tell Den I said that."

Lindsay snorted.

Meg ordered her drinks. "You should join us. Den's been telling stories about you. You might want a right of reply."

Lindsay resisted the urge to roll her eyes. Den had a way of building Lindsay up to almost mytholog-ical proportions. And although Lindsay knew she was a good goalkeeper, she was never a braggart.

Meg persisted. "She's got the whole team convinced you were some sort of super goalkeeper."

Lindsay glanced over Meg's shoulder. Den and some others in Mustangs tracksuits were pulling tables together, making space for everyone. Pop was already in the thick of it, chatting happily with anyone who'd listen.

Lindsay collected her drinks and followed Meg to the table, bracing herself. She could handle Pop's post-training chatter, but being ambushed by Den and her coaches? That was going to test her patience.

The chatter at the table was a low buzz as Den and Pop talked about training, and Den's coaches at the other end of the table talked amongst themselves, writing in notebooks and glancing at tablets. The mood was upbeat, which wasn't surprising given the team were one game away from a grand final trophy and automatic entry into what sounded like the biggest club tournament in the country.

Talk turned to the goalkeeper, Ellie. Pop said "Confidence issue" when Den asked him his opinion. "And poor communication."

Den leaned back in her chair as a server placed her food in front of her. "I don't know how to change that. We work on visualisation and the mental game. She still looks shaky."

"Something outside could be going on," Pop said. He glanced at Lindsay, who knew only too well what 'something outside the game' could mean. The table had gone quiet as plates of food were delivered. Lindsay cut into her steak and pretended to ignore the conversation.

"She just needs to toughen up and take charge," a coach from further down the table said. Lindsay glanced up, noted the stoney look on Meg's face and that she had taken a great interest in her parmigiana, and then turned her head to see who had spoken. The coach continued, puffing out his chest slightly. "In my day, we didn't have time for keepers with confidence issues. You either commanded the box or you were out. Simple as that. Ellie hasn't got the temperament to lead the back line. Grace, on the other hand, won't take a backward step."

"Grace doesn't have the skills yet, Gary," Den said, her voice measured.

Gary huffed. "The board seems to think she does. They've made their preference clear. They want a leader in the box, not a project."

Lindsay cut her steak just a little more aggressively than normal. He sounded just like another coach Lindsay used to know. One she'd rather forget. "Or maybe the problem isn't her temperament or maturity. Maybe someone's giving her reasons to not trust her place in the team."

Meg's fork paused half-way to her mouth, and Den raised an eyebrow but said nothing. The coach blinked at her and huffed and went back to his tablet, ignoring everyone around him.

Lindsay stood up. "I need to get another drink."

"I'll come with you," Den said, pushing away from the table.

When they reached the bar, Lindsay said, "That coach sounds like a piece of work."

Den's expression softened. "I know what you're thinking. But the game's moved on from coaches like Wickham."

Lindsay's jaw tightened at the mention of his name. She could still hear his barked criticism in her head, his snide comments about being a failure, as sharp and as clear as if it were yesterday.

"Seems to me they're still around," she replied, nodding toward the table where Gary sat with his tablet.

"Yeah, well, unfortunately for me, Gary's a board pick," Den said. "I'm stuck with him until his contract runs out. Which is why I need your eyes, Linds. You should come to the game tomorrow. See Ellie in action for yourself." She turned and leaned her elbows on the bar, nodding to the table. "I can tell you what I see, but you always had a knack for spotting things the rest of us missed."

Lindsay signalled to Craig for more drinks. "I told you, I'm out. I have a business to run."

"One game. That's all I'm asking. Just watch her. Nothing more."

"I've got work tomorrow," Lindsay replied.

Den gave her a look that said she wasn't buying Lindsay's excuses but she didn't argue. "Well. The invite's there."

Craig placed their drinks on the bar and before Lindsay could argue, Den paid for them. "Consider that a sweetener," she winked.

"Pop's in his element," Craig said.

"Yeah, he is," Lindsay replied. She picked up her drinks and weaved her way back to the table.

FOUR

The next afternoon, Lindsay pulled her ute into a parking bay as close as she could get to the main gate. Blue and gold Mustangs flags and bunting were strewn on the buildings near the entrances and, Lindsay noted, there were more people than she thought would be here for a women's match. Before she could get out of the car, Pop was hauling himself out of the passenger side.

"Jesus, Pop, you'll do your back again," Lindsay roused.

"I wouldn't if you'd drive my damned car," Pop groused right back.

"It's a death trap," Lindsay countered. "And I'm sure you'd—"

"—rather be alive than dead," Pop finished. "Sometimes I wonder."

Lindsay smirked as she closed the door behind him. "Got everything?"

Pop checked his backpack and patted his pockets. "All good. I'll see you inside."

It wasn't a question, and when Lindsay didn't answer, he turned to the kids waiting near the gate. "Lindsay's coming, too," he called. The kids cheered.

Lindsay rolled her eyes. It wasn't that she didn't like the kids. She liked them perfectly fine. It was just that they played a game Lindsay would rather stay as far away from as possible these days.

"I'll park the car and I'll meet you inside," Lindsay said, watching as her Pop shuffled off to the entrance gates, answering the million questions his under nines team had for him. Her heart swelled as she watched them disappear inside. He was the reason she had started playing in the first place. It was a pity that his love for the game wasn't enough to convince her to keep playing once she'd decided to stop.

She got back into her car and found a park three bays away, which meant she'd have to bring the car around to pick Pop up after the game. And that meant a later afternoon than she'd hoped, but it wouldn't bother Pop. He'd spend every spare minute at the grounds if he could.

As she entered the grounds, her phone buzzed. *'Message not sent'*.

Lindsay opened her messages. The last three to Rod had pinged back. She dialed his number and got a busy signal. Frustrated that he was now seemingly avoiding her, she shoved her phone into her pocket and entered the grounds.

The stands were filling up, a sea of blue and gold and green and white flags and shirts and bunting. There was a low buzz that tugged at Lindsay's memories from long ago. This was bigger than the crowds they used to get at finals. She dodged some kids running along the front of the main stand and scanned for Pop and the kids.

She found them at the top of the stands, just as she'd expected. He'd drilled into her from a young age that the best place to watch a match was from the nosebleed seats. No doubt he was instilling that same wisdom in his current team.

Lindsay was half-way up into the stand when someone called her name from below. Lindsay turned to see Meg shielding her eyes from the sun.

"Denise said you can sit in the team stand behind the bench if you'd like." Meg's energy practically oozed out of every pore. It wasn't surprising, given the importance of today's game to her club.

"I'm good," Lindsay said taking a step up.

"If you're sure?" Meg said. "I get the feeling Denise wants you close to the sideline so she can chat."

"I'm sure," Lindsay replied. "And you can tell Den that she should just be glad I came."

Meg's smile faltered a little, making Lindsay feel bad.

"I can see the game better from up top," Lindsay explained, softening her voice. "I'll catch up with her after the game."

Meg nodded. "Okay. I'll let her know."

When Lindsay took a seat beside Pop, he asked, "What did Meg want?"

"Den wants me to sit with her."

"Easier to see everything from up here," Pop said.

Lindsay wriggled on the hard plastic seat, trying to get comfortable. "That's what I told her."

"Here they come!" one of Pop's players called. The kids jumped out of their seats and cheered as the Mustangs players ran onto the field alongside their opponents, Southside United who, according to Pop, made the final from fourth spot. No mean feat.

Lindsay stayed seated and trained her eyes on the Mustangs goalkeepers who began warming up at one end. There were two of them, but Ellie, the one she'd seen on the DVD, was obviously first choice, judging from the way she was being warmed up by the other one.

Spotting nothing out of the ordinary, Lindsay waited for the game to start to see if anything jumped out at her. She hoped not, but if there was, she'd tell Den so she could sort it out, and that would be the end of it.

FIVE

THE GAME WAS END-TO-END in the first twenty minutes, but eventually, Den's Mustangs wrangled control through maintaining possession much longer than Southside. It took thirty-five minutes for them to score, but once they did, it was like the floodgates opened. Chances came and flew wide or off the cross bar for the remainder of the first half.

Lindsay glanced at the bench every now and then to check Den's reactions. While Den was passionate about the game, she was measured on the sideline. She couldn't sit still, pacing up and down in the box, but she didn't yell or call out much. Just watched and wrote in her notebook, and occasionally chatted to the subs and other coaches.

One coach, however, was extremely vocal. Gary. He gestured wildly at the players when they knocked the ball out for a corner.

It was also apparent that the players could hear him, Ellie the goalkeeper, especially. Every time Lindsay heard Gary's voice, Ellie did a neck stretch and a shoulder shake. It was like a tic. Something she'd let Den know about when she saw her after the game. Not about the tic, but that it was a reaction to the coach.

"Watch their seven," Lindsay said to Pop. She'd spotted a pattern over the last ten minutes and wanted to see if Pop saw it too. Every time play shifted to the right, the Southside winger on the opposite side would drift away from her marker, and then make a hard, diagonal run behind the Mustang's left back. Classic blind spot play.

"Good run," Pop said. "They just need a good cross."

Lindsay pulled out her phone and pulled up Den's number. *Southside #7 is making blindside runs behind your FB on the outside. Wide open for the switch.* She hit send.

A moment later, she saw Den pull her phone from her jacket pocket. Den read the message, and then she turned her head, scanning the stands until her eyes met Lindsay's. Lindsay gave a short, sharp nod, confirming it. Den nodded back, slipping her phone away.

A few moments later, during a stoppage in play, Den called her midfielder over for a drink. She spoke to her briefly, gesturing towards the space Lindsay had identified. The midfielder nodded, ran back onto the field and spoke to the fullback.

For the rest of the half, the fullback diligently tracked back, shutting down the winger's run. Southside tried to switch the play twice, but both times the pass was easily intercepted.

At half-time as the teams headed off the pitch and into the change rooms, Den glanced up at Lindsay and gave her a thumbs up.

In the second half, the Mustangs kicked up a notch, running Southside around the park and scoring four more goals. Lindsay didn't have much more to go on for Den's goalkeeper. She rarely saw the ball for most of the second half.

Then, late in the second half, the Mustangs lost possession in the back line when the left back passed across goal for a switch, and a Southside striker swooped in and stole the ball off the toes of the centre back. It was a mad dash for the centre and outside backs, chasing back to the 18-yard box, trying to regain possession.

Lindsay leaned forward in her seat, watching Ellie, waiting to see what she'd do.

Ellie set herself, then started to move forward shutting down the angle for the impending one-on-one. Out of nowhere, the right back ran across attempting to make the tackle, leaving Ellie in no-man's land with no ability to make a save. The Southside striker toed the ball forward, past Ellie, who could only make a feeble attempt at a save.

While Southside celebrated the consolation goal, Ellie was left to retrieve the ball from the net and punt it to her forwards for a kick-off.

Lindsay could tell from her body language that something was definitely not right.

Although the team celebrated at the final whistle, Ellie's celebrations felt muted. She was smiling, but it didn't quite reach her eyes, and while she jumped around with her team mates, it wasn't as energetic and free-wheeling as everyone else.

Lindsay recognised that look. It was the quiet shame of a player who blamed herself, even when it wasn't her fault. The pressure had gotten to her, and even though her team won, she carried that goal like a loss.

After getting signatures and photos with the players from both teams, Pop and his team kicked a ball around on the edge of the field while they waited for their parents to pick them up, and Lindsay made her way down the tunnel to the change rooms.

She hovered outside, listening to the muffled noise seeping out from behind the doors. She knew exactly what it would smell like in there, and she wasn't sure if she wanted to go in.

The door swung open and Meg bustled out, the bucket she was carrying stopping her from running directly into Lindsay. The noise of celebrations from inside intensified.

"Oh! Sorry," Meg said.

"Oh, no. My fault," Lindsay replied.

Meg's smile lit up her entire face. It was disarming and… cute. And when Meg's eyes flicked over her, a hint of colour rising in her cheeks, Lindsay realised she wasn't the only one who noticed.

Then Meg blinked, back to business. "You can go in," she said. "Denise is expecting you."

Lindsay peeked over Meg's shoulder into the room. "Actually, could you just let Den know I'm outside. It's probably easier to hear each other out here."

"Sure," Meg replied, smiling. She went back into the room, and Lindsay moved across to the other side of the tunnel and leaned back on the wall. It had been a long time since she was in a change room, and just the thought of it made her feel slightly queasy.

The noise from the room grew louder again as Den walked through the door, Meg after her and heading down the tunnel.

"We're through," Den said, grinning. "That was a good spot on their winger, by the way. Thanks for the heads up."

Lindsay shrugged. "I wasn't watching the winger. I was watching your goalkeeper, who, from what I can see, is lacking in confidence."

"That's it?" Den asked, surprised.

"What do you want me to say? It was one game."

Den nodded. "Okay. So nothing technical then?"

"Not that I could see today. But the backs don't trust her. That last goal was a pretty big indicator that something's not right with them. Your right back could've injured your goalkeeper coming through like that. You might want to get them running some drills together to get that sorted. And there's something going on with Gary. Every time your keeper heard him from the bench, she stretched to release some tension."

"I'll take that under advisement," Den said. "Thanks." She turned to leave but then turned back. "You should come and help us celebrate."

"I have to get Pop home," Lindsay replied.

"Right," Den said.

Meg returned with a bucket full of ice. "Sorry. Ice run," she said, disappearing into the change room.

Den cocked her head. "You know, we have a pre-tournament camp in a month. Before our first Champions League game. You should come with us."

"Nope," Lindsay replied. "One game, you said. That's what I gave you."

"It's just like our old rep camps, only much nicer rooms to stay in," Den said with a grin.

"I hated our camps," Lindsay deadpanned.

"You did not," Den laughed. "And anyway, you can be an assistant coach. I'd even pay you."

"I'm not a coach," Lindsay said.

"Pop said you have your certification," Den countered. "You can put it to good use."

"Still doesn't make me a coach," Lindsay said.

They stood looking at each other for a moment until Den said, "You're going to make me do it, aren't you?"

"Do what?" Lindsay asked.

Den pulled a face. "I'm calling it in."

"Calling what in?" Lindsay asked. She had a moment of realisation. "Oh, no you're not."

Den stepped closer. "Oh yes, I am. Lindsay Ruth McAllister I am officially calling in the Captain's Oath."

Lindsay dragged her hands down her face. "Oh for— Den, that was a stupid oath we made when we were kids. It doesn't mean anything."

"It meant something to us then, Linds. 'Always answer the team's call, no matter what.' Remember?"

Lindsay did remember, but right now, she just wanted to forget it. "You can't hold that over me now."

Den cocked her head. "Can't I?"

"It's not even my team," Lindsay argued.

"No, it's my team," Den agreed. "But I'm *you're* team, and that makes this your team too."

"No that's— not even a thing," Lindsay said, exasperated.

"Then why are you still arguing with me?"

Lindsay pushed off from the wall and walked away. "Congrats on the win."

"The team needs you," Denise called after her. "And you'd really be helping me out."

Lindsay didn't stop walking. She just waved over her shoulder. "Good luck for the tournament."

As she exited the tunnel, she laughed to herself. Captain's Oath? Den had rocks in her head.

SIX

A WEEK LATER, AS Lindsay was getting ready for work, she got a text from an unknown number.

Hi Lindsay. It's Ops Manager Meg. I'm organising the pre-tournament camp. Denise wanted me to check if you were coming or not. Let me know ASAP.

Lindsay's lips twitched despite herself. Trust Den to send the Ops Manager after her. She rolled her eyes at Den's persistence. There was something about seeing Meg's name on her screen that made her pause for a second longer than she should have before typing her reply. She sent back a polite decline and shoved her phone into her pocket.

She poured herself a coffee, padded into the lounge room and sat down beside Pop who had the newspaper opened on his lap, the morning news on the TV in the background.

"What's on today?" Pop asked, not looking up from his newspaper.

"I need to finish the wood chip at Eldridge Park," Lindsay replied. "I shouldn't. Rod still hasn't paid me. And I still can't get onto him."

"Then take the day off," Pop said not looking up.

Lindsay drank her coffee. Pop knew she'd finish the job regardless. She looked up at the TV where a 'breaking news' banner flashed on the screen. She turned up the volume and listened as the reporter detailed the collapse of Murchison Developments. Lindsay felt the blood drain from her face. Pop dropped the newspaper into his lap and turned his attention to the TV.

"Isn't that—"

"Rod's boss," Lindsay finished. The coffee turned to acid in her stomach as she listened to the reporter detailing the millions of dollars in debt and the contractors and small businesses left without incomes. Lindsay's business was one of them. "Shit."

Lindsay's phone rang. She answered, but was too stunned by the news to check the caller or answer it properly, and just said "Hello?" It was Rod.

"Lindsay, I'm so sorry. I only just found out too."

"Where are you ringing from?" Lindsay asked. It wasn't his usual phone number.

"They cut off everything," Rod said. Lindsay could hear the despair in his voice. "I don't know what to do. I'm so sorry."

Lindsay stood up and walked into the hallway, turning so she could still see the TV. "What have they said to you? The company."

"Nothing," Rod said. "I called a few other blokes and they said the same thing. None of us have been paid in weeks. Some of us for months. It's a bloody nightmare."

"Wait a minute," Lindsay said. She covered the phone. "Pop, turn it up." There was a graphic on the screen with the name and phone number of the receivers. The reporter said that anyone who had a creditor's claim should contact them. She took a photo with her phone. "Did you see the graphic on the news just now?"

"I missed it," Rod said.

"It was the name of the receivers. I'm sending you a photo now. We need to contact them."

"Okay," Rod said. "Okay. Thanks. We'll get this sorted, Linds, I promise."

"Just… go deal with your stuff, and I'll deal with mine."

They hung up, and Lindsay went back into the lounge room and picked up her coffee cup. "Looks like I'll be taking the day off after all," she said.

Lindsay surfaced again for lunch after spending hours on the phone to the receivers and then trawling through receipts and invoices and scanning and cataloguing them to email them. They couldn't guarantee Lindsay would get much, if anything, once they were finished winding the company up, because Lindsay was a small fish in the very big pond of commercial construction.

When she sat down at the kitchen bench with her sandwich and a glass of water, she was exhausted. Pop ambled in and asked, "So what now?"

"I go to my old client book and start ringing around, I guess," Lindsay replied. "No idea how many will take me back but it'll be a start."

Pop rinsed his glass in the sink. "You're not twenty anymore, Linds. You'll burn yourself out doing those jobs again."

"I have to do something," Lindsay replied, a bit angrier than she intended. "I need to find some way to pay my suppliers out."

"There is another option," Pop said.

"What option?"

Pop smiled and raised an eyebrow. "Coaching with Denise. Maybe it's time you took some time out, took a step back, get your head right so you can sort the business out properly."

"I'm not going on a soccer camp," Lindsay said.

"Why not? It's not like you have any work on now."

Pop was joking, Lindsay knew that, but there was more to her business than the actual physical work.

"What's the worst that could happen?" Pop pushed. "Your paperwork will still be here when you get back. And it will probably take months for those lawyers to sort out Murchisons."

Lindsay let out a breath. "What about you?"

"I'm quite capable of looking after myself, despite what you think," Pop said. "And when was the last time you took some time off, for yourself?"

"Playing assistant coach wouldn't be taking time off," Lindsay replied.

"It would be time off if you treated it that way," Pop countered. "Soccer is a game, Lindsay. It's not meant to be serious."

"It's serious for them," Lindsay said. "They're paid to play now. It's their job. It can't be fun."

She heard those words come out of her mouth and remembered how fun the game was for her until it wasn't, and why.

Pop leaned on the bench and crossed his arms. "Denise needs you. And if that cranky coach Gary is anything to go by, that goalkeeper needs you, too."

Lindsay scoffed.

"You've been in her shoes, Linds. Think about what it would have meant if someone had stood up for you back then? Where would you be now?"

"Not standing here on the verge of losing my business, that's for sure," Lindsay mumbled.

Pop stepped across the kitchen and stood in front of Lindsay. Lindsay had a flashback to the first time she realised she stood as tall as him when she was fifteen. He'd shrunk since then, and Lindsay had grown, so he had to look up at her, but his eyes were intense. He grabbed her arms. "Linds, you loved the game once. I know you still have it in you. You saw the potential in that 'keeper, just like I did. I know you did. Are you going to let her fall away like you were allowed to?"

"I'm not her saviour, Pop," Lindsay snapped. "And I'm not Den's, either. My business is all I've got and I'm not walking away from it to go and play on a stupid soccer camp."

"Lindsay—"

"Drop it, Pop." She dumped her plate in the sink and stormed out.

SEVEN

Lindsay rolled out her shoulders as she pulled off her boots at the front door. It had been two weeks since Murchison's collapse, and she'd spent every day since grinding through underpaid and physical odd jobs just to stay afloat. She pulled off her sweat-soaked socks and checked her heels. Another blister to add to her collection. She hadn't had blisters since she was an apprentice with Rod.

She followed the smell of beef stew through the house to the kitchen and found Pop sitting at the table, glasses on, reading the newspaper. She ducked into the laundry and tossed her socks into the laundry basket, rinsed her hands in the sink and then grabbed a beer from the fridge.

"You look like you've been dragged through a hedge backwards," Pop said, chuckling.

Lindsay flopped into a chair opposite him, her work shirt sticking to her back with sweat. "Four cash jobs in one day will do that."

"Cash jobs don't pay the bills," Pop said, turning the page of his newspaper.

Lindsay was too bone-tired to argue, but the truth was, Pop was right. She was barely keeping her head above water. She rubbed her hands over her face. "Murchison's still owe me ten grand. If I don't do something, I'll go broke."

Pop set the paper down and gave her the look that silenced the junior teams he coached for decades. The one that said *don't argue, just listen.* "And how long do you think you can keep this up?"

"As long as I need to," Lindsay muttered, taking a long drink of her beer. She leaned back in her chair, stretching her legs out in front of her, trying to relax. She tipped her head back and closed her eyes.

"You do have another option, love," Pop said, his voice softer.

Lindsay didn't look up. "If you say Denise Baker, I swear to God—"

"I'm just saying. She's been trying to reach you. You haven't been answering your phone."

"Because I don't want to talk to her." Lindsay placed the beer bottle on the table a little harder than she meant to. The phone calls and messages were still there on her phone, unanswered. Den asking if she'd reconsider. Den offering to cover her fuel or pay for her bus ticket. Den reminding her *I'll pay you*. Den reminding her about their stupid Captain's Oath.

Pop took his glasses off and leaned on the table. "She believes you can help her win the tournament. I think she might be right."

Lindsay scoffed. "Leave my business to fail to run off to a soccer camp? Brilliant plan, Pop."

He ignored her sarcasm. "Your business is failing, love," he said gently. "The camp could be a good chance for you to start fresh. Work out what to do next. And that keeper, Ellie, she needs someone like you. Don't tell me you didn't see yourself in her."

Pop knew all the right buttons to push, and sometimes she hated him for it. She hated it more that he was usually right. She chewed on the inside of her lip. It was ten days. Not even that, since they were already in Toowoomba. So, a week, maybe. And depending on how much Den was offering to pay her, the money might give her some breathing space to work out how to rebuild her business.

She picked up her phone and opened Denise's message. She started typing.

How much are we talking?

Denise's reply came back in a flash. *$3,000*

"Three grand," Lindsay mumbled to herself, but Pop caught it. It would take her a month to earn that sort of money the way she was going right now.

"See? Nothing to sneeze at. And much better money than wrecking yourself gardening."

She stared at the number on the screen until it blurred. Three grand was hard to ignore. It was enough to cover some of her overdue invoices. Enough to buy her some time. She blew out a long breath.

When do you need me there? She pressed send before she had second thoughts.

Denise's reply came back in a flash. *Meg will send you the details. Make sure you check your emails for once.*

"This'll come back to bite me," she muttered.

"You'd regret not going more," Pop said.

EIGHT

It had been three weeks since the Murchison's collapse. With her business stalled, Lindsay stepped off the bus in Toowoomba, into the world of the Mustangs. Whatever happened next, at least she wasn't at home watching her business crumble around her.

Outside the bus station, she messaged Pop to let him know she'd arrived safely and that she'd call him in the morning. He replied with a thumbs up. She cursed the day she showed him how to use emojis, and pocketed her phone.

She looked up to see Meg leaning against an SUV plastered with Mustangs logos and sponsors.

"You drew the short straw, huh?" Lindsay joked as she strode across to the car and tossed her bags into the boot.

"I offered," Meg replied, brushing a strand of hair behind her ear before settling into the driver's seat. Something about the casual motion stuck in Lindsay's mind and she turned away, forcing her gaze out the window so she didn't stare too long.

As Meg steered them out into traffic, she asked, "Have you had dinner? The girls have all been fed and watered and are currently doing video analysis."

"I could eat," Lindsay replied, her stomach in knots. Maybe it was hunger, or maybe it was the thought of 'video analysis' that turned her stomach.

Meg took a right at the traffic lights. "Don't tell anyone, but I'm going to take you to a place called Cholesterol Corner."

Lindsay snorted. She had a fair idea why Meg offered to pick her up now. Meg appeared to have a secret fast food fetish.

"You can pick your poison," Meg continued. "Only thing is, we'll have to dine in. Joey can smell fried food a mile away. He's our team nutritionist, and he'll be wanting to put you on a plan as soon as he gets a chance. He does that for everyone, including the staff."

"How does fast food fit into your plan?" Lindsay asked.

"It doesn't," Meg replied. "And that's why we're never speaking of this to anyone."

Lindsay smirked. If Meg was willing to sneak fast food past the team nutritionist, maybe Lindsay had found her first ally.

They drove along the main road to the west, neon fast food signs lighting up the night on both sides of the road. Meg wasn't kidding. Every fast food place, big, small and local, was accounted for. In the end, they both chose a local burger joint. Lindsay ordered a fried chicken burger and Meg made sure Lindsay tried some of her chips which she declared the best fast food chips in Queensland hands down. They grinned as they ate their contraband meals at a table outside the restaurant so they didn't get the smell in the car.

When Lindsay reached over to swipe another chip, her fingers brushed Meg's. Meg jerked her hand back. "Sorry."

"They're your chips," Lindsay said, one eyebrow arched.

"You're right," Meg said, swiping the chip out of Lindsay's hand and popping it into her mouth.

"You did offer, though," Lindsay said. She grabbed for another one and Meg pulled the box away.

They both laughed before Meg pushed the box back. "I suppose you can have one more."

"Just one?" Lindsay asked.

"We'll see," Meg replied.

The forbidden fast food run did its job, and Meg's easy chatter left Lindsay feeling unexpectedly relaxed. Maybe even optimistic. Just a few days, she reminded herself for the millionth time. A few days to help Den with whatever she needed, to clear her head, and then get back to business. She could totally do this.

The SUV slowed as the motel came into view, and Lindsay's brief window of calm slammed shut. She wasn't here to relax. She was here to walk into a world she'd once run from, full of people she didn't know, and a role she was yet to understand.

A massive sign in the lobby of the motel welcomed the Mustangs to the Garden City. It was nice to see a women's team being celebrated and welcomed. In

Lindsay's day, no-one cared who they were or what they'd won or achieved.

Meg helped Lindsay check in at reception and as they turned to head to the elevators, Den appeared. "Lindsay! Just in time. We're heading to the conference room to chat about the intra-squad game. Can you join us?"

Lindsay glanced at Meg who waved her off. "You go. I'll take your things to your room."

"Are you sure?" Lindsay asked. She didn't want to take advantage of Meg's apparent urge to help.

"I'm right next door, so I'm heading that way anyway."

"Okay," Lindsay replied. "Thanks."

"No problem," Meg called after them as Lindsay fell into step with Den.

"Maccas or Hungry Jacks?" Den asked as she led Lindsay down a carpeted hallway.

Lindsay sniffed her shirt, thinking the smell of fast food had stuck.

Den laughed. "It's a pretty open secret around here. Even Joey knows."

Lindsay let out a half laugh and rolled her eyes. "Busted," she said.

Den paused, her hand on the conference room door. "Don't you tell Meg everyone knows, or I'll send you back to the coast."

Lindsay snorted and followed Den into the room. A round table was set up in a corner of the room, around which sat Den's coaching staff. Den introduced them one by one, officially this time, and they all shook Lindsay's hand or gave her a wave or a nod. They seemed like a pretty good bunch. The only one missing was Gary.

Lindsay listened as they talked about player work rates and fitness and other stats that she felt didn't really matter. They watched some game footage from previous games that the coaches used to pitch targeted drills for upcoming training sessions.

As talk shifted to tomorrow's game, Gary strolled in late and dropped into a chair like he owned the place. "Sorry. Family stuff," he muttered, immediately pulling out his phone and tapping on it. He didn't acknowledge Lindsay, or Den for that matter, apart from the curt apology.

"Right," Den said, not acknowledging the apology. "Let's move on to who's going to start in the back line for the A squad tomorrow." She brought a pitch map up on the screen with players' names in their positions. She had a three-player back line, which was different to the grand final, and five in the midfield. Lindsay was intrigued.

Gary, however, took immediate affront to the goalkeeper. "Grace should get a start in the main squad. She's been training well and, I think, will command that back line better, especially if you're going to run three instead of four."

"Ellie's starting," Den said flatly.

Lindsay got the feeling this wasn't the first time they'd butted heads over goalkeepers. Den didn't argue. She just moved on.

"We'll move Fi into a central defensive midfield role to see how she goes. I'd like to see what she can do with a bit more freedom—"

"With all due respect, if Ellie can't trust her back line, then maybe she's not cut out to be our last line of defence."

"Or maybe it's the back line's job to back her up," Lindsay said before she could stop herself.

Gary shot her a glare and raised his hand dismissively. "She's not part of the coaching team," he said to Den. Not talking directly to Lindsay was meant to make her feel small and insignificant.

"Lindsay will be my direct assistant until the end of camp. Her opinions and ideas will be treated with the same respect as anyone in this room."

Gary opened his mouth like he was going to argue, but Den shut him down. "You've made your position clear. Let's move on."

Den let a silence hang in the air. Lindsay wondered if it was a dare to Gary to argue back. Instead, he leaned back in his chair and crossed his arms, but didn't say anything more. Lindsay noted the way the other coaches either looked down at their notebooks and tablets or kept their eyes on the screen. She wondered if this tension was transferring to the team.

There was a more constructive discussion around who would play in the midfield and up front, with Den making two changes to her preferred starting lineup based on player workload concerns, and a player whose usual position was in defense was given a chance up front in the B squad to see what she could do based on the advice of the attacking coach.

By the time the meeting was over, it was close to 11pm. Lindsay wasn't sure she'd last the week if every pre-game strategy meeting was going to be the same. She'd known physical exhaustion, and that was bad enough. The mental exhaustion of thinking so much about minute details of the players and the team and the opposition, that would tire her out completely.

Gary was the first to leave the conference room, walking at a pace that told Lindsay exactly how pissed off he was. The other coaches chatted with each other in pairs and groups as they collected their gear and headed up to their rooms. One coach, Mike, nodded at Lindsay. "You've made an enemy, you know."

Lindsay shrugged. "I get the feeling he's got plenty of them."

Mike laughed. "I'm looking forward to working with you, even if he isn't."

"Thanks," Lindsay replied. She hung back, waiting for Den to finish a chat with one of the team analysts. Finally, with just the two of them left, Den walked Lindsay to the door and said, "Drink?"

"I'm knackered," Lindsay replied. "I should get some sleep so I'm fresh for tomorrow.

Den nodded as they stepped out into the hallway. "Fair enough. You should have a schedule in your room. Meg will probably want to give you the full run down first thing, so maybe catch up with her for breakfast."

Lindsay hit the button when they reached the elevators.

Den added with a sly smile, "If you don't, she'll be scheduling a 'friendly check-in' before you've had your first coffee. And if you miss that…"

Lindsay chuckled. "Let me guess. She'll ambush me in the hallway with a clipboard?"

The elevator dinged and the doors slid open. They stepped in and rode up in comfortable silence.

When the elevator stopped at Lindsay's floor, she stepped out and turned to Den.

"Are you sure you want me here? I'm not exactly sure how much help I'll be."

"Tonight proved how much I need you," Den said. "Your soccer brain is exactly what I've been missing." She paused. "It's good having a friendly face around the place."

"That I can do," Lindsay said with a smile.

As the doors began to slide shut, Den added, "Don't skip breakfast. That's when Meg's at her most dangerous."

Lindsay laughed. "Noted," she said, then unlocked her door and stepped into the darkened room.

She flicked on the light. A Mustangs-branded folder sat neatly on the desk, a sticky note stuck to the cover:

7am breakfast in the motel restaurant. Will run through your contract and schedule over coffee —Meg

Lindsay grinned and shook her head. Meg was efficient. Thoughtful, too. She needed a shower, then she'd check her work emails, and hopefully get some sleep.

NINE

Lindsay pushed through the restaurant doors to a sea of blue and gold uniforms and a low buzz and clink of cutlery and crockery as the Mustangs ate their breakfast. She felt out of place in her jeans and t-shirt, but she didn't own any tracksuit pants and she hadn't been given a uniform.

She scanned the room and spotted Meg sitting in a booth in a corner, drinking from a large mug. Lindsay guessed it had to be coffee, figuring that Meg's energy had to be fueled by caffeine.

Lindsay tucked her schedule under her arm, wandered by the food stations and grabbed herself a bowl of warm rolled oats with brown sugar and a splash of milk. She poured herself a mug of coffee, and weaved her way through the dining room to Meg's booth.

"Morning," Lindsay said as she slipped into the seat across from Meg.

Meg looked up from her folder, reading glasses perched on her nose, and a smile entirely too big for this time of the morning. "Good morning!" she said.

Lindsay wondered how much coffee Meg had consumed already.

"How did you sleep?" Meg asked.

"Pretty good, actually," Lindsay replied.

Meg nodded at Lindsay's bowl. "Joey will be impressed with your breakfast."

"I figured I should make a good first impression," Lindsay replied.

"If you really want to impress him, make sure you add some fruit to it tomorrow," Meg replied with a wink.

"Why would I ruin good porridge with fruit?" Lindsay joked.

Meg chuckled. "Ready to get started?"

Lindsay took a sip of her coffee. It wasn't the best she'd tasted, but it was caffeine, and she figured she was going to need it, judging by the colour-tabbed folder Meg had open in front of her.

"First things first," Meg said. "We need you to look part of the team. You'll see on today's schedule that we have you listed for a uniform fitting after breakfast. We have two more rookies coming on board with us today, and you. All three of you will stay here and get fitted for your training and formal uniforms while the team goes through their gym session. You'll be expected to wear official team uniforms for the duration of the camp, including to meals and any excursions."

Lindsay nodded and drank more of her coffee.

"I've spoken to Denise this morning. She'll explain more to you when she sees you, but essentially, your role is to shadow her while you're here, and report anything you think needs attention or tweaking."

Meg flipped to another page and pulled out a page filled with neat stripes of highlighter. She took it out of the file and slid it across to Lindsay.

"Your mornings will mostly consist of strategy meetings and on-pitch coaching blocks. You don't need to attend the gym sessions, unless you want to get in some gym time yourself."

She glanced over her glasses with a look Lindsay couldn't quite read, but it could have been flirty. Lindsay forced herself to nod, like she was listening intently. In reality, she was trying to ignore the little spark that flared when Meg looked at her like that.

Meg continued. "Afternoons will be training or recovery sessions, player reviews, or media duties, which you won't really have to worry about. Today, it's an intra-squad match. We've got a free day tomorrow, a down day for the players to have some time off, and then a clinic on Thursday. That's an important one. The club want lots of positive attention on the team leading into the Champions League tournament." She paused, flicking a page up at the corner. "Oh, and Denise wants you sitting in on tonight's post-match analysis. You might need caffeine for that one. They'll be discussing the tournament team, and they tend to run late."

"That sounds like a lot," Lindsay said, eyeing the dense schedule.

"Welcome to the pros," Meg said, grinning. "Just remember, it looks scarier on paper. You'll get into the rhythm pretty quickly."

She slid another piece of paper across with a 'sign here' sticker placed neatly next to a line under where Lindsay's name was typed. "This is the contract for your temporary role. You can see here—" she pointed with the tip of the pen. "— this is your remuneration for the camp. I'm sorry I can't negotiate anything more for you. We've used some of our discretionary funds to pay you so the board doesn't have to approve it."

Lindsay wanted to tell Meg that three thousand dollars was more than she'd expected for a few days' work, but she didn't.

"And here," Meg said, placing a coloured form on top of the contract, "are your tax forms. Can you fill them in when you get the chance today? I need to get them and your contract to HR by tonight if I can."

Lindsay sucked in a breath and let it out. Signing these forms would make it real.

"Ready to become a Mustang?" Meg asked.

Lindsay read over the brief contract, picking at the corner of the page with her fingernail. *Was* she ready to become a Mustang? She re-read the start and finish dates on the contract again. It was less than a week, she reminded herself. And she'd be getting three grand for essentially being a friendly face for Den and maybe helping a young goalkeeper keep her spot in the team.

She signed the contract and handed it back.

"Welcome to the team," Meg said grinning.

In the conference room, tables were spread full of blue and gold Mustangs kit, and some temporary change rooms were set up beside them. Meg waved Lindsay over when she spotted her and introduced her to their kit manager, Liam, who proceeded to pull clothes from the table and hand them to Lindsay.

"Liam is going to get you out of your jeans and t-shirt comfort zone and into Mustangs chic," Meg said, her eyes twinkling.

Lindsay resisted the urge to roll her eyes. "There's nothing wrong with jeans and t-shirts." She wondered if Meg had anything between the Ops Manager corporate wear and Mustangs team kit, the only two things Lindsay had seen her wearing so far.

"Medium in most things I'm guessing," Liam said, looking her up and down several times as he grabbed training shorts, track pants, and a track jacket. "How do you like your shirts to fit?"

"I prefer some room," Lindsay replied.

"Me too," Liam said. "Most of the girls prefer fitted these days. No idea why. I couldn't think of anything worse." He handed Lindsay a club polo and a training shirt. "Jump in one of those booths and try them on. If you want to swap out sizes, let me know."

As Lindsay pulled the curtain closed, two players entered the room. They must be the rookies Meg mentioned at breakfast. They looked like they were still in high school. Lindsay listened to their easy chatter as she tried on the team kit, marveling at how accurate Liam was with his sizing estimates. It was his job, she figured, so it made sense he was good at it. She pulled open the curtain. "What do you think?" she asked Meg.

"You look like an assistant coach," Meg said, glancing up from her clipboard, her head tilting slightly. Her eyes swept over Lindsay in a way that made her pulse skip.

"Thanks," Lindsay replied, feeling slightly self-conscious. She didn't know whether that was because of the 'assistant coach' title, or the way Meg's eyes seemed to linger, appraising more than the club kit. She removed her jacket to reveal her club polo. "Not too big?" she asked.

"Whatever you're comfortable in," Liam replied, pulling Lindsay's attention away from Meg. He picked kit for the two rookies and sent them into the other change rooms. The girls chatted to each other as they changed, completely oblivious to the adults in the room.

Liam looked Lindsay up and down and nodded. "You pass," he said. "Take off your kit and head over to Penny who will heat press your initials on.

"You didn't tell me I'd get a personalised kit," Lindsay said to Meg as she stepped back into the change room.

"Lots of perks in this job," Meg replied with a wink.

As Lindsay changed back into her jeans and t-shirt, she thought about how easy Meg was making things for her. It was probably why she got her job. She did wonder whether Meg was as accommodating with the other staff, or whether being Den's friend got her extra special treatment.

Lindsay pulled back the curtain and headed over to Penny, who with a nod and a smile, proceeded to heat press LM on Lindsay's uniform.

Meg bounced over, crossing things off her clipboard and checking her watch. "You've got a half hour to get changed into your training kit, and then

I'll take you and the girls to the field for the gym session."

Lindsay nodded, watching as Penny pressed the final letter into place. Her initials, clear and permanent. It felt official now. More official than she'd expected.

She gathered up her new kit and gave Meg a half-smile. "Guess I'd better start acting like an assistant coach."

She headed out of the room, feeling the weight of the uniform in her arms, and something else she hadn't felt in a long time. A little glimmer of excitement.

TEN

HALF AN HOUR LATER, dressed in their new club kit, Lindsay and the rookies arrived at the stadium via Meg's SUV to catch the end of the morning's gym session.

Lindsay felt the music before she heard it, the heavy bass thrumming through the floor as she pulled open the door of the gym. Meg had shown her where to go but left Lindsay on her own to finalise paperwork, and a reminder about the strategy meeting at lunch.

The rookies pushed through the door first, voices nervous with energy. Unsure where to go, Mike directed them to a weights station with some of their team mates.

Lindsay leaned on the door frame, taking in the players in groups at different stations, putting in more hard work than Lindsay ever had.

"Last set! This one's for bragging rights!" Mike yelled over the music. He stalked across to a station where players were swinging kettle bells. "Push, push, push!"

Even though he was yelling instructions, Lindsay could tell the difference between Mike's tone and Gary's anger. Mike's pushing was good-natured and motivational. Gary's was designed to tear players down. She knew a coach like that once. He'd told her his job was to break her down and build her back up. All he did was break her.

Lindsay scanned the room, her eyes finally finding Ellie at the squat rack with Grace and another player. Ellie was just coming up from a squat, slowly but surely, and racked the bar. She grinned as Grace and the other player high-fived her. Interesting too, Lindsay thought, that the competition for spots hadn't translated to a competitiveness off the field between Ellie and Grace.

Mike spotted Lindsay, grinning when he saw her, but not missing a beat with his motivation. "One more set and we're done," he yelled with a wink at

Lindsay. A chorus of groans broke out around the room.

"You just said that," someone called out.

"We need to see what these rookies can do," he yelled, circling his finger in the air. "Switch it up!"

The players moved stations, and got set up and ready. Mike counted them down and checked his watch. "Ready? In three-two-one… let's go!"

The players all began their exercises, the low buzz of chatter and laughter drowned out by the music, still pumping loudly, setting the rhythm so that a lot of the players were strangely in sync.

Lindsay stayed watching until Mike called time, the girls collapsing in heaps on the mats.

"Let's get out of here and get showered and go have some lunch," Mike called as he switched off the music. The girls grabbed their bags and gear and trailed out down the tunnel. Lindsay waited behind to walk with Mike.

"Do the girls always have so much fun in the gym?"

Mike scoffed. "That looked like fun?"

"Not to me," Lindsay said with a laugh. "But the girls looked like they weren't complaining."

Mike shrugged his bag over his shoulder. "If I don't make it fun, they'll hate it and won't want to do it."

Lindsay nodded. 'I wish I'd had that,' she thought to herself.

"They know working hard makes them play better," Mike continued. "But keeping it fun will keep them engaged longer. It helps with team bonding as well." He opened the door to car park, stepping aside so Lindsay could go ahead of him.

For Lindsay, team bonding was less about weights and drills and more about games arcades and impromptu touch footy at the beach. She wondered if that old arcade she'd visited with her rep team years ago was still open.

"Are you coming on the bus with us?" Mike asked.

Lindsay glanced across at Meg who was on her phone. "I'll catch a ride with Meg."

"No problem." Mike waited until all of the players were on the bus before he got on.

Lindsay wandered over to Meg, who held up her hand to let Lindsay know she'd be a minute. When she hung up, she turned to Lindsay and smiled. "What did you think?"

"They work a lot harder than I did when I played," Lindsay said. Meg started walking towards the car, and Lindsay followed.

"They have to. It's so competitive for spots now," Meg said.

"It's always been competitive for spots at that level," Lindsay said, clicking her seatbelt in. "I've just never seen girls their age do so much physical work just to kick a ball around a field."

"Well, for some of them, kicking that ball around a field is a dream they're willing to do anything for," Meg said, pulling the car around behind the bus, waiting for them to leave.

Lindsay remembered that feeling. But she also remembered the feeling of that dream being ripped from her grasp. She shook off the memory.

"Hey, is there any chance I can get some match footage?" she asked. "I wouldn't mind seeing Ellie and Grace in action during the season."

Meg followed the bus out of the stadium. "Look at you doing homework."

"Well, it is my job, apparently," Lindsay joked.

Meg grinned. "Yes, it is. I'll get our analyst, Pete, to send you some through."

"Thanks," Lindsay replied. If she could see how Ellie played earlier in the season, maybe she could see what Den saw.

ELEVEN

Lindsay had to skip the strategy meeting to deal with business emails. She called Pop while she had some time up her sleeve, just to let him know how she was going. He was at his team's end-of-season break-up when she called. She could hear the laughter and squeals of the kids in the background. She smiled despite herself, remembering her own junior club break-ups. That was probably the last time she could remember really enjoying playing.

By the time she was finished, she'd missed the bus to the grounds. Meg, dependable as always, Lindsay was discovering, was waiting for her in the motel foyer.

"You're going to have to take the bus at some point," Meg said.

"Oh I don't know. I kinda like having my own personal Uber driver," Lindsay replied.

Meg grinned. "As long as you give me a five star rating."

"I might even give you an extra tip," Lindsay joked.

Meg laughed, an easy genuine laugh that warmed something in Lindsay she hadn't expected.

When they arrived at the stadium, Lindsay headed down into the change rooms, while Meg took a phone call outside, saying she'd be in soon.

As Lindsay walked down the hallway, she heard muffled voices. When she got closer, she realised it was Gary's voice.

"You want to be first choice? Then stop playing like you're scared of the ball. Keepers don't get sympathy. One mistake and you cost us the game. That's it. You think Denise is going to pick you if you crumble under pressure?"

A small hesitant voice - Ellie's - said, "I...I'm trying. I just--"

"Trying isn't good enough," Gary snapped. "Grace commands her backline. You? You freeze. And if you freeze in a game what do you think is going to happen?"

Lindsay's fists clenched at her sides. Taking a player away from the group to berate her? What did he think that was going to achieve?

There was a heavy silence before Gary lowered his tone. "You've got one chance to prove you're worth that shirt."

Footsteps faded away and she rounded the corner to find Ellie leaning against the concrete wall, her head tipped back, eyes closed, arms limp at her side. She looked absolutely deflated.

"Hey," Lindsay said. Ellie jumped. "Sorry, I didn't mean to scare you."

Ellie pushed away from the wall and turned away.

"Hey," Lindsay said again. "You know all of that is bullshit, right?"

"He's right" Ellie replied. "Grace is better. She should be goalkeeper, not me." She started to walk away. Lindsay rushed to catch her up.

"I've seen you play," Lindsay said. "In the final."

Ellie [illegible].

"You read the game better than you realise. I'm not surprised Denise signed you."

Ellie crossed her arms. Silence again, but she was paying attention now.

"You're good, Ellie. Better than you give your-self credit for."

"I'm not great though. That's what Gary wants."

"You're what, twenty?"

"Nineteen," Ellie corrected her.

"You're practically a baby," Lindsay said.

Ellie rolled her eyes.

"What I mean," Lindsay said, "is that you still have a lot to learn. But from what I've seen, you have natural instincts. You can't coach that."

Ellie bit her lip. The door down the hall-way opened, and players started filing out of the change room and heading down to the field.

"Do you want the number one spot or not?" Lindsay asked.

Ellie nodded.

"Then you're going to have to fight for it," Lindsay said. "Shut Gary out. I know that's hard. I've been there."

Den exited the change room and glanced down the hallway. She cocked her head at Lindsay who gave her a thumbs up and called, "We're coming."

Den nodded and followed the team out to the pitch.

"Listen," Lindsay said. "You don't know me and what I've done, and I'm probably overstepping my mark, but I can tell you I've been right where you are. Right now? You need to go out there and play your own game, using your own instincts. Are you going to make mistakes? Yes. But it's how you learn from them that counts. Soccer is a team sport, Ellie. Us goalkeepers always play with the weight of the world on our shoulders, but we have ten other team mates to rely on."

"I know that," Ellie said in that unimpressed tone that teenagers seemed to have just for adults. "Wait. You were a goalkeeper?"

Lindsay was getting more personal than she wanted, but right now, Ellie needed someone on her side. "I was exactly where you are now, and I walked away." She paused and took a breath. "I ended up hating the game. I don't want that for you."

"I might not have a choice. Gary doesn't think I belong in the team," Ellie said, her voice pained.

Lindsay knew she had to get Ellie to think about her game differently, or she was going to prove Gary right. Lindsay was determined not to let that happen.

"Okay, look," she said, trying again. "You know what I used to do to get out of my head?"

Ellie shook her head.

"I focused on my team mates. Every time someone else on my team did something good, I told them. Hey, today? Even do it with your opposition. They are your team mates. And really celebrate Grace's saves."

"Why would I do that?" Ellie asked.

"Because despite everything else, Grace is your squad mate. You need her to have your back. From what I saw of you in the gym, she's not competing with you the way you think she is."

"Ellie! Come on!" Gary's voice carried down the hall.

"Remember what I said," Lindsay said as Ellie jogged down the hallway.

Lindsay watched her go, hoping she could shut Gary out, just for today.

"You sound like a coach," Meg said from behind.

Lindsay spun around. "How much of that did you hear?"

Meg shrugged, a smile tugging at her mouth. "Enough."

"I just don't want Ellie to end up like me," Lindsay replied softly.

"Oh, I don't know," Meg replied, her eyes glinting. "I think she could do worse than helping her team win five grand finals in a row with her penalty-saving heroics."

Lindsay blinked. "You've been talking to Den."

Meg leaned closer, her elbow brushing Lindsay's in a gentle nudge. "I'm the Ops Manager. It's my job to know who we're hiring."

The casual nudge made Lindsay's pulse skip. She told herself Meg was only being friendly, but the tingle on her skin left her wondering if it could be something more.

TWELVE

Ellie started the game off quietly, unsure of herself, glancing up to Lindsay in the stands as if asking for permission. By the half-hour mark, she was clapping and calling out to her team mates, and good plays from the opposition. Lindsay took great delight every time Gary muttered "What the fuck is she doing?" whenever Ellie praised a team mate or the opposition.

It wasn't long before Gary let his frustration get to him. From the sideline, he yelled at a defender for not stepping up quickly enough. "Wake up! You're giving them too much space!"

A moment later, a simple pass came toward the defender and instead of trapping it cleanly, she took a heavy touch, the ball bouncing away from her and intercepted by an attacker. It forced a panicked scramble from the rest of the defense.

When Grace made a spectacular one-handed diving save, cleaning up the mess, Ellie was the loudest on the field. Gary whipped around and fixed Lindsay with a glare as if the whole play had been her fault. She shrugged and clapped harder.

Grace was still much more vocal than Ellie, but Ellie led with her positioning and quiet chats to her defense. They were chalk and cheese with their personalities, but Ellie was starting to show some of the instincts that got her the contract. Grace, while confident, got some calls wrong, and was out of position on a few occasions. Through it all, though, Ellie's voice carried across the field, encouraging and positive.

When they stopped for half-time, Lindsay jogged down the steps to grab Den and pull her aside. "Don't let Gary take the keepers away from the team."

Den gave her a funny look, but nodded. The squad huddled in the shade, drinking from water bottles and listening to the coaches. When Gary said, "Can I grab Grace and Ellie for a chat?" Den refused.

"Actually, I think we'll just do a full squad chat if you don't mind."

Gary opened his mouth to protest, but Den plowed on, not letting him talk. Interestingly, as the teams filed back onto the field, Grace and Ellie walked on together side-by-side, laughing and giving each other friendly shoves. Lindsay smiled to herself.

The second half was pretty much the same as the first, with coaches moving players around between the teams to test strategies and combinations. Grace's voice mirrored Ellie's more positive tone, and both goalkeepers played well in the second half.

When the game was finished, Den pulled Lindsay aside. "I don't know what you said to Ellie, but that was the most relaxed she's played."

"I just reminded her why she was here," Lindsay replied with a shrug.

"I told you you could coach", Den teased. She clapped Lindsay on the shoulder, and jogged ahead to talk to some of her assistant coaches. As they reached the tunnel, a hand grabbed Lindsay's arm and swung her around.

"What the hell do you think you're doing?" Gary.

"My job," Lindsay said bluntly. She turned to head back into the tunnel.

"You're just here as an emotional support dog to Denise," Gary spat. "She's going to make this team an embarrassment."

Lindsay spun on her heels, took two steps into Gary's space and eyeballed him. "You're not a coach," she said. "You tear people down and call it development. Maybe that's why you never made it as a player."

Gary's eyes darkened, and Lindsay knew she'd guessed right. He leaned in and lowered his voice. "You have no idea who you're dealing with."

"No, I don't," Lindsay said. "Because you're no-one to me."

Gary's jaw twitched and Lindsay thought he was going to bite back. Instead, he said, "You're done" and stepped around her, knocking her shoulder with his as he stalked down the tunnel to the change room.

Lindsay stood for a moment, her heart beating hard and fast. She took several deep breaths through her nose and out through her mouth to calm herself. Meg's head appeared around the change room door. "Are you coming in this time?"

Lindsay plastered a smile on her face. "I'm coming."

Her heart was still hammering in her chest as she made her way down the tunnel, wondering how she was going to survive the rest of camp with him.

The motel restaurant was too chaotic and loud for Lindsay's liking after the afternoon she'd had, so she ordered room service instead. She carried her plate of steak and vegetables out to the balcony and sat at the small glass table, looking out over a manicured park. The lamp lights were just starting to turn on in the early dusk, and despite the cooler air, there were people out in droves wandering through the park or biking or zooming along the paths on e-scooters.

A truck laden with garden rubbish was parked near a brick building, two hi-vis-clad workers packing up for the day beside it. A pang of homesickness hit her. A brief moment of yearning for the simple monotonous routine of shovelling and spreading mulch or trimming hedges.

Her gardening work back home was so uncomplicated, she hardly had to think about what she was doing. At least it was uncomplicated until Murchison's went bust. She'd done as much as she could with the receivers, and now she just had to wait it out. And while she did that, she had to spend the next few days trying to help Den get the best out of a goalkeeper who was being hamstrung by a terrible coach.

She sliced into her steak, loaded up on vegetables and shoved them in her mouth. At least the steak was good.

She thought she'd left soccer behind, yet here she was, right back in the thick of it. A lot of things had changed, but a lot of things had stayed the same. Case in point: Gary. She didn't know how people, men, like him, kept getting jobs coaching women.

There was a tap at her door, so light that Lindsay wasn't sure she'd heard it. She padded across the carpeted floor and peered through the peep hole to see a fish-eyed Meg standing in the hallway. Her heart quickened as she opened the door.

"Hey," Meg said. "I didn't see you at dinner so I thought I'd come and check on you."

"Oh, I'm good. Thanks," Lindsay replied.

Meg shifted on her feet. "So, Mike had a word to me about Gary."

"Oh?"

"Did he threaten you today?"

Lindsay knew how this conversation might go. Knowing she wasn't going to be here for long, and not knowing how much influence Gary had over the team and coaches, she decided to brush it off. "We had a difference of opinion," she said.

"You're sure?" Meg asked.

Lindsay shrugged, hoping she sounded convincing. "He's just blindsided by my being here, that's all. I don't blame him, really."

Meg looked unconvinced. "If you're sure."

"I'm sure," Lindsay said.

"Okay then." Meg half-turned to leave but her feet didn't move. "Um, well, I was going to go for a drive, to check out some sights, since we have free time now until tomorrow afternoon, and… I wondered if you might like to come with me? You don't have to, obviously. If you have other plans. But I could do with the company."

Meg was babbling. It was cute. More than cute, if Lindsay was being totally honest.

"Is this a fast food run?" Lindsay teased.

Meg cocked her head, and Lindsay's chest gave a little squeeze. Why did that have to be so adorable? "There may be a quick stop at Maccas."

Lindsay grinned. "In that case, I'm in. Just let me grab my jacket." She went to her wardrobe to grab her leather jacket and then wondered if this constituted an official team trip. She called back to Meg, "Team jacket or civvies?"

"Civvies," Meg called back. "We're off the clock."

Lindsay pulled her leather jacket on and closed her door behind her. "Oh really? I'm looking forward to seeing what an off-the-clock Meg gets up to."

Lindsay swore she saw Meg blush and she had to admit, if Meg had asked her to go and watch the paint dry on a wall, she probably would have said yes.

THIRTEEN

The view from Picnic Point across the Lockyer Valley towards the east was spectacular. Car lights trailed down the mountain towards Brisbane, where the lights from the city shimmered in the distance. A cool breeze drifted through the trees, making Lindsay pull her jacket tighter.

Meg chose a bench seat with views across the valley, and Lindsay settled in beside her, the McDonald's bag nestled between them. As Lindsay dug into her sundae, Meg said, "How was your first official day?"

Lindsay ate slowly, giving herself time to think. "Interesting," she said finally. There were a few other words she could use, but she still didn't know Meg well enough yet. Her main priority was to support Den, and now Ellie and Grace. Coaches like Gary thrived on conflict, and Lindsay wasn't going to overstep her mark when she was only temporary.

Meg apparently picked up on Lindsay's reluctance, because she changed the subject. "Den said you have your own landscaping business."

Lindsay stole one of Meg's fries, dipped it into her ice-cream, and popped it into her mouth. "I do. Well… I did."

Meg bit into her burger and glanced sideways at Lindsay, her eyes questioning. Lindsay licked her lips, set her sundae on her lap and sighed.

"I put all my eggs in one basket, and now the basket has gone bust. The truth is…" She hesitated, the words heavier than she expected. "The truth is, the business is gone. I keep telling myself that I'll get through it, but I can't. It's finished."

Saying it out loud, after trying not to think about it the last couple of days, felt like ripping off a band aid.

Meg's expression softened. "What happened? It's okay if you don't want to tell me. I'm way too nosey for my own good sometimes."

That made Lindsay smile. "You're the ops manager. Isn't it your job to know everything?"

Meg chuckled and shook her head. "Sometimes I wish I didn't have to."

Lindsay looked out over the ridge, the stream of headlights and taillights glowing in the night. "I subcontracted for a major developer, let go of my small jobs, because the pay was better. And now the developer is in receivership. I'm not sure how I'm going to pay my bills." She wrinkled her nose and let out a breath. "It's a mess."

"I'm sorry," Meg said quietly.

"It is what it is," Lindsay replied, forcing a half-smile. "Honestly? I needed the money. And maybe some time away to figure out what comes next." She blew out a breath. "Plus Den pulled the nuclear option. She called in the Captain's Oath."

Meg paused mid-sip. "The what now?"

"The Captain's Oath." Lindsay shook her head. "Super serious stuff when you're seventeen. Basically, if the team, or each other, ever really needed us, we'd answer the call. No questions asked."

Meg's eyes twinkled in the low light. "And she actually used it?"

"She did," Lindsay replied. Then she shrugged, as if that explained everything.

She let the last thought hang in the air for what seemed like ages. Finally, she discarded the empty sundae cup in the bag and leaned back on the bench, tipping her head to the sky, as if the answers were in the stars.

"Last time I was in Toowoomba was for State titles when I was fifteen," Lindsay said quietly.

"So you were good back then?" Meg joked.

Lindsay gave Meg a side-eye glance. "If you'd asked me back then, I would have told you I was the best."

"Now?" Meg prodded.

Lindsay drew in a breath and exhaled slowly. "Now? I'd probably still say I was the best."

Meg's laugh bubbled up, infectious, and Lindsay found herself grinning.

"Den said you were humble," Meg teased.

It was Lindsay's turn to laugh. She enjoyed how easy Meg was to talk to. She could see why she was so good at her job.

"Do you and Den talk about anything else other than me?" Lindsay teased back. She swore Meg's cheeks coloured, but it could have been a trick of the light.

Meg looked away. "Well, we do talk about Mike and Joey, but the conversations about you are a lot more fun."

Lindsay's heart skipped, a warmth winding its way around her body against the chill night. Was Meg flirting? She found herself hoping she was.

Meg cleared her throat. "So… if you've been here before, you could show me what the gardens look like at night."

Lindsay grinned. "Sure. I need to walk off that sundae anyway."

They binned their rubbish, and Lindsay led them down towards the waterfall, lit up to the night, the rush of water drowning out most of the low traffic buzz coming from the highway on the range.

They leaned on the fence, a spark of electricity shooting between them when their arms brushed. Lindsay felt like a teenager again. Awkward and lost for words all of a sudden. She was saved from embarrassing herself when Meg's phone rang.

"Sorry," Meg said. "Oh, it's Den. I should probably get it." She picked up and said a cheery hi, and then her face darkened. "Okay. Yes, we're coming back now."

"Everything okay?" Lindsay asked as they walked back to the car.

"Staff issue," Meg said, her lips in a tight line.

Lindsay didn't push, and they drove in silence back to the motel, the mood heavier.

Den was waiting for them in the motel foyer, arms crossed, jaw tight.

"I'll see you in the morning," Lindsay said, turning towards the elevators.

"I need you too," Den said, cutting her off.

Lindsay trailed after them into a small conference room, unease tightening her chest.

Den dropped into a chair, motioned for them to sit, and dragged a hand down her face before looking directly at Lindsay.

"I want you to tell me what happened today with Gary," she said.

Lindsay's first instinct was to say that nothing had happened, but she had a feeling Den wouldn't be asking if she didn't already know some of it.

"Which part? The one where he takes players away to berate them in private? Or the part where he called me your emotional support dog?"

Meg sucked in a breath. Den didn't flinch.

"Tell me about before the game. With Ellie in the tunnel," Den said.

"I overheard Gary getting stuck into Ellie before the game. You know my thoughts on that," Lindsay said, her voice even. "I don't care if it's part of my job or not. I'm not going to let a grown man speak to a young woman like that."

"What did you say to Gary at that time?" Den's voice gave nothing away.

"I didn't say anything to him. When I turned the corner and saw Ellie upset, Gary was heading back to the change room."

"Okay," Den said. "What did you say to Ellie?"

"I just told her she was better than she thought, and gave her some tips to get out of her own head."

Den nodded and glanced down. "Gary has accused you of undermining his coaching."

Lindsay shook her head. "Typical."

Den leaned in. "Now tell me about the confrontation you had with Gary after the game."

Lindsay shot to her feet. "Are you kidding me? You asked me to help you out but if your coaches don't want me here, then I may as well go home."

"Sit down, Linds. This is about Gary, not you."

Lindsay hovered for a moment, hands balled tight, until Den nodded at the chair.

"Please, Linds." Den drew in a tired breath. "Meg, depending on what Lindsay tells me, I will be asking you to recommend disciplinary action for Gary."

Meg pulled out her phone. "I'll need to take some notes." She tapped on the screen and placed it on the table. "Do you mind if I record? I may need proof for my recommendation."

Lindsay dropped back into her chair and waved her hand. "I don't have a problem with that."

"Okay," Den said, the formal tone back. "I've had some concerns brought to me tonight that I want to get to the bottom of. Meg, I think you'll find that they are a continuance of previous concerns around some of our coaching staff."

Meg nodded. Lindsay realised that this probably wasn't the first time Gary had been reprimanded.

"So. Tell me everything that happened with Gary today, especially what you overheard with Ellie."

Lindsay recounted what she'd overheard in the tunnel, her conversation with Ellie, and then her clash with Gary after the game. Den and Meg interrupted periodically to clarify details, and by the end of it, she was drained.

She stood, stretching out the stiffness in her back, and headed for the door.

"I'll see you in the morning," Meg said. "Den and I have to discuss what you've just told us."

Lindsay nodded. She glanced at Den. "If I'm making things harder for you, or the other coaches, I can go home."

Den smiled tiredly. "You're not going anywhere, Linds. The positive impact you have on players is obvious. I need more of that."

Lindsay nodded. "Okay. Well, I'm going to have a stiff drink before bed. I'll leave you to it." She turned for the door.

"You should make it a double," Meg said, her tone light and her eyes soft. "You've earned it."

Lindsay glanced back. Meg's expression was unreadable, but there was a hint of a smile tugging at the corners of her lips and a glint in her eyes. Lindsay felt her chest loosen just a little.

In the elevator on the way up to her room, Lindsay realised that despite offering to go home, she actually wanted to stay.

FOURTEEN

MEG AND DEN WERE nowhere to be seen at breakfast the next morning, and Lindsay hadn't had so much as a text or email from them about the night before. She had turned off her alarm, deciding to sleep in for the first time in years, and by time she got down to the restaurant for breakfast, only a few players were scattered around the tables, talking and laughing.

Lindsay ate in silence, sipping her coffee, thoughts of last night's meeting with Den and Meg turning over in her head. Den wanted her here, that much was clear, but if she was more distraction than help, then heading home might be better for everyone.

Her thoughts turned to her conversation with Mike and how he made hard work look like fun. Hadn't she said the same thing to Ellie just yesterday? Maybe she should take her own advice. Maybe a bit of fun would shake her out of the heaviness that had settled since last night.

On a whim, she pulled out her phone and searched for the old arcade she'd spent time in with her rep team a lifetime ago. It was long gone, but in its place was a giant TimeZone arcade located in the shopping centre. It probably wouldn't be the same as that dusty old arcade from her youth, but maybe some old-fashioned fun was just what she needed to shake off yesterday's drama.

She could hear the arcade before she saw it, the whoops and dings and sirens indicating winners permeating the third floor as Lindsay arrived at the top of the escalator.

Stepping inside took her back to almost thirty years ago, running around with her team mates, trying to beat each other at Pacman, pooling spools of tickets to win the biggest prizes. Now they had cards you inserted into the machines to count your wins. She was a bit disappointed that today's kids wouldn't have the sheer joy of carrying around massive spools of little paper tickets and dumping them on the prize counter for a pimply teenager to have to count them one-by-one.

She wandered around for a few minutes, taking in the sights and sounds and trying to decide which machine she'd try first. Most of the games were different to what she remembered from her childhood, but there were some classic pinball machines hidden in corners.

As she wandered around, she spotted the unmistakable blue and gold jackets of some Mustangs players. She avoided them, figuring they wouldn't want a coach spoiling their fun. More players were dotted around the place, and it seemed like she'd discovered where half of the team had decided to spend their free day. As she headed to the claw machines, she spotted Ellie and Grace, laughing together at a shooting range game.

She stepped back so they couldn't see her, but was interested in the way they interacted and had fun together. Ellie looked like she had shaken off yesterday's run in with Gary which was good to see. They elbowed each other, high-fiving, laughing.

Lindsay smiled to herself, glad that despite everything she'd seen yesterday, the two players seemed to still be tight. She turned around and continued wandering until she found what she was looking for - the basketball toss. She took a free lane, swiped her card, and watched the game clock count down. On the green flashing light, she started tossing basketballs at the hoop, swearing under her breath every time she missed one. She'd gotten rusty. This, and any of the reaction games, were her specialty back in the day.

She finished round one with 18 baskets and was about to press start for a second round when a voice said, "I think I might have discovered something you're bad at."

Lindsay laughed and turned to see Meg standing behind her, arms crossed, head cocked.

"I'm just warming up," Lindsay said.

"Oh yeah?"

"Yeah," Lindsay said, tossing Meg a ball. Meg, quick as a wink, caught it without flinching and stepped forward.

"You don't know who you're dealing with." She tossed the ball back to Lindsay.

Lindsay watched as Meg stepped up to the lane beside her and swiped her card. "Loser buys lunch?"

"Oh you're on," Lindsay grinned. "I don't eat cheap, by the way."

The machine blared the countdown, lights flashing, and Lindsay felt her chest loosen. She sneaked a glance at Meg who turned to look back at the exact same time. Their eyes locked, and Lindsay felt heat curl low in her chest. From the flicker that crossed Meg's face, she wasn't the only one caught off guard.

Lindsay was so lost in the moment that she almost missed the start buzzer. Meg didn't, though, and had sunk 2 baskets before Lindsay had even had her first shot. Lindsay laughed as she picked up the balls and started shooting. For the first time in a long time, she wasn't thinking of cancelled contracts or her run-in with Gary or how much she was supposed to hate soccer. She was totally focused on the ball in her hands, and Meg's infectious laughter and friendly jibing beside her.

Meg swiped a fry from Lindsay's plate and dabbed it in tomato sauce. "These are so bad for you."

"That's what makes them irresistible," Lindsay countered.

Meg grinned and glanced around. "I'd forgotten how much fun these places could be."

"Me too," Lindsay said. She leaned back in her chair. They'd decided to eat at the TimeZone cafe, right in the middle of the arcade, lights and buzzers and sounds all around them. Kids ran ahead of their parents from game to game, and they spied the occasional blue and gold jacket or shirt of the players. They tried to avoid them, giving them their space, knowing how seeing coaches could kill their fun.

"You know these are like casinos for kids?" Meg said.

Lindsay laughed. "Why do you say that?"

Meg turned in her chair to survey the room. Her blonde hair flashed red, blue, red from the lights of a nearby game and Lindsay had to remind herself to concentrate on the conversation instead of the way the lights played across Meg's face. "Can you tell me where we came in?"

Lindsay glanced around. "The dodgems are over there," she said pointing to her left. "And the big

Whack-a-mole is over there." She pointed straight ahead. "So…. That means the claw machines are that way, which is where I came in. I don't know about you though."

Meg grinned. "There are four entrances if you count the escalator that goes up into the cinema above us. And every entrance has claw machines."

"Huh," Lindsay said, impressed.

"They're designed to make it hard to find your way back out. Just like casinos," Meg said with a satisfied grin.

Lindsay narrowed her eyes as she ate a chicken nugget. "How do you know this stuff?"

"I did my dissertation on how games arcades can be a precursor to gambling addiction," Meg replied. "Specifically, how reward-based environments shape behaviour. Riveting stuff."

"Oh my God, I didn't realise you were a nerd!" Lindsay joked.

Meg tossed a chip at Lindsay, landing on her plate. Lindsay ate it with a grin, but the warmth curling through her chest wasn't from the food. It was the ease of sitting here, bantering with Meg, like they'd known each other for years.

It occurred to Lindsay that neither of them had mentioned Gary. Although she wanted to know what had happened since last night, she didn't want to break the spell between them and ruin the moment.

Meg suddenly stood, a glint in her eyes. "Right, McAllister. I'm thinking about a nice steak dinner tonight at your expense."

Lindsay pushed back from the table and stood up. "I am not going to lose twice."

"We'll see about that." Meg strode off, tossing Lindsay a look that made following feel less like an option and more like a dare.

FIFTEEN

After laughing their way through pinball, racing games and shoot'em ups, Lindsay's eyes landed on a game she couldn't resist. The Reaction Ring. On instinct, she caught Meg's hand and pulled her along. The warmth of Meg's skin against hers registered a second later, sending a jolt through her. She should have let go, but Meg's fingers stayed curled against hers, and Lindsay found herself reluctant to break the connection.

They stood, hand-in-hand, watching a man try and fail to catch all the sticks as they fell. Lindsay should have been studying the mechanics of the game, but her mind was fixed on the warmth of Meg's hand in hers. Oh god, had Meg just brushed her thumb across the back of her hand? Heat climbed

Lindsay's neck and she swallowed hard, forcing herself to concentrate on the game.

"This is what you're willing to lose a steak dinner over?" Meg teased.

"This is my bread and butter," Lindsay shot back.

Meg's laugh bubbled out, warm and unguarded. And still, she didn't let go.

Finally, the man's turn was over, and Lindsay had to let go of Meg's hand to step up to the game. She picked up the sticks from the floor where the man had left them and connected them to the ring above her head. She read the instructions, which amounted to 'catch the sticks before they touch the ground', and let out a breath. Quick reflexes were her calling card back when she was playing, and they hadn't dulled too much over the years. At least she didn't think they had.

She swiped her card and rubbed her hands together. "Let's do this," she mumbled to herself as she pressed the button to start the game.

The sticks dropped randomly, at differing intervals over 30 seconds, and she managed to catch two from ten on her first attempt.

"I'm really looking forward to that steak," Meg teased. "I think I might get the wagyu."

"That was just a practice," Lindsay said, wiping her hands on her track pants. She rolled her shoulders and stretched her neck. "Right. Let's go." She pressed the green button and set her stance, knees slightly bent, arms out in front, hip height. She fixed her focus on a point on the centre of the ring, letting the edges blur until all ten sticks were in her peripheral vision.

The countdown flashed.

Three.

Two.

One.

The first stick dropped. Her hand shot out, snatching it before it hit the floor. She almost celebrated, but the second stick fell and then the third from the opposite side. Her instincts, honed over years of training and playing in goal, kicked in, the sounds of the arcade dulling around her as she caught each stick, one by one, until one remained.

She heard Meg's voice beside her, encouraging her on but remained focused on the lone stick remaining. It fell almost in slow motion. Lindsay lunged, closing her hand around it before it touched the ground.

The sounds of the arcade rushed back in and she brandished her fists full of sticks in triumph like she'd just saved a penalty in a world cup final.

Meg said, "Okay so I guess dinner's on me."

"That was just level one," Lindsay said. She set the sticks back in place. "What do I get for winning level two?"

Meg put her finger to her lips, thinking. "I guess I could spring for dessert."

Lindsay grinned as she turned back to the game. "This one's for creme brulee."

"Really? I would have guessed you'd be a tiramisu girl," Meg said.

"Stop trying to distract me," Lindsay joked as the timer counted down.

The sticks dropped marginally faster this time, but Lindsay swiped the first three, and then almost missed the fourth. She got down to the ninth again and waited for the tenth. And waited. And waited. Just when she thought the machine had broken, it dropped, and Lindsay lunged forward, juggling it with her left hand, flipping it into the air and grabbing it with her right.

She turned, triumphant, to see Meg grinning and clapping. Behind her was a sea of blue and gold jackets, the players cheering and whistling.

"Go coach!" a voice said from behind. Lindsay swung around to see Ellie and Grace clapping and grinning.

Lindsay held out the sticks to Ellie. "Let's see what you've got."

Ellie pointed to herself and mouthed 'me?' and Lindsay nodded. Grace shook Ellie's shoulder, egging her on. Ellie stepped forward and took the sticks from Lindsay, placing them back into place. Her team mates crowded around behind her, cheering her on.

Lindsay and Meg stepped back and gave the girls room, watching as Ellie scored six in her first attempt. Grace stepped up and managed three. Another player stepped up, the three of them laughing and shrieking as she fumbled the sticks, the crowd of Mustangs team mates cheering them on.

Meg leaned into Lindsay, her voice low, "So what if we split the steak, and I buy the dessert?"

"Are you renegging on our bet?" Lindsay asked, one eyebrow cocked.

"You'd hardly call your first attempt a win," Meg countered.

"I was just warming up," Lindsay said, nudging Meg's shoulder with her own.

"There's no warm-ups in bets," Meg said with a wink.

"Fine. Dinner, which we split, and you shout dessert," Lindsay said. She hesitated, then added before she could stop herself, "Sounds like a date."

"It does," Meg said, her eyes twinkling.

Lindsay blinked, thrown off balance, surprised by her own boldness, and Meg's ease at accepting it as a date. Ellie's triumphant whoop saved her from having to respond.

Meg looped her arm through Lindsay's. "Come on. Let's leave the girls to their fun. We've got important business to attend to. Like deciding where to go for dinner."

SIXTEEN

The dinner date was put on hold while Meg dealt with the fall-out from the Gary situation. Lindsay still didn't know what was happening, but whatever it was, she was sure she'd find out eventually. She decided to call her Pop to check in.

"The kids are going to a tournament next weekend," Pop said. "I can't go because I have an appointment on Friday."

"Do you need me to come home?" Lindsay asked.

"I can look after myself," Pop replied. "Last time I looked, I was an adult too."

Lindsay smiled at Pop's sassiness. "If you need me, let me know. I'm only a couple of hours away."

"How is coaching?" Pop asked, changing the subject.

Lindsay paused, thinking about the last couple of days. "It been interesting."

"Good interesting?" Pop pushed.

"A lot has changed since I was playing," Lindsay admitted. "They track everything electronically now, and they've got a coach for everything."

Pop chuckled into the phone.

Lindsay opened the balcony door and stepped outside into the early evening twilight. "Most of the coaches have been supportive," she continued. "Meg, the ops manager, has been great. She's… organised, but not in that bossy way. Like…" Lindsay dropped into a chair. "You wouldn't even know she's really the boss here. And she always seems to know what people need before they do. She even--"

Lindsay stopped herself, heat prickling her neck. "Anyway, she's good at her job."

Pop chuckled. "Sounds like you've found a friend."

Lindsay picked up on the emphasis on 'friend' and heat crept up her neck again. Is that what Meg was? A friend? Friends didn't hold hands at the arcade, unless they were twelve-year-olds, which Meg and Lindsay definitely were not.

"What about the players?" Pop asked. "How's our goalkeeper, Ellie, doing?"

Lindsay loved how he spoke about the players he'd come in contact with.

"I... think I may have made a bit of a difference to her game," Lindsay said tentatively. "But it's gotten me offside with the coach. I don't think he's happy I'm here."

"Well, you can't help that, love. You know how teams work. And as long as you're helping Denise."

Lindsay smiled. "I know, and I think I am. But this is different. Anyway, I don't want to talk about one shitty coach. What have you been up to since I've been gone?"

"Mrs Radcliffe popped in for morning tea and said to say hello. Oh, and I pruned those roses out the front."

"I could have done those when I got home," Lindsay said.

Pop ignored her and plowed on. "And I planted those pumpkin seeds you left on the newspaper."

"Pop..."

"You're busy, Lindsay," Pop said. "I'm quite capable of doing the gardening."

Lindsay shook her head. "Can you at least leave something for me to do when I get home? I don't know if I'll have a business to work in when I get back."

"You shouldn't talk like that, love," Pop said, his voice insistent. "Just concentrate on soccer for now, and whatever the business looks like when you get back we'll deal with."

There was a knock at her door. "I have to go. I'll ring you tomorrow."

"Okay, love. Have fun!"

Lindsay hung up the call and opened her door. Meg was standing there holding a plate covered with a cloche. "Room service," Meg said, grinning. She lifted the cloche to reveal two creme brulees.

"What about our dinner date?" Lindsay asked, stepping aside.

"Oh, I'll still hold you to that," Meg teased as she stepped past Lindsay into the room. "In here, or balcony?"

"Balcony," Lindsay replied, closing the door and following Meg out.

They settled into the chairs on the balcony, cracking into the brulees as the streetlights flickered on and the night air cooled around them. Meg pulled her knee up to her chest, spoon in hand, looking comfortable in a way that made Lindsay's heart swell in her chest.

For a while, it was just sweet, creamy dessert and gentle ribbing about their arcade game rivalry. Then Meg's phone buzzed against the table. She silenced it, but the flicker in her expression told Lindsay that maybe Meg needed something light and sweet right now too.

Meg withdrew into herself for a moment, and Lindsay let her, not wanting to burst the bubble that seemed to surround them in that moment. She wanted it to last just a little bit longer, the two of them alone on the balcony, easy in each other's company, not feeling the need to talk.

Finally, Meg turned to Lindsay and said, "Gary was given a formal warning and put on restricted duties."

Lindsay leaned back in her chair. "Wow. How did that go down?"

"About as good as you can imagine," Meg replied with a tired smile. "It's been a day."

"Is it because of me?" Lindsay asked. "Because—"

Meg held up her hand to stop Lindsay from continuing. "It's been coming for a while."

Lindsay let out a breath. "How's Den?"

The corner of Meg's mouth twitched up. "You know Denise. Getting on with things."

Lindsay gave a half-smile and glanced down at the floor, kicking at a loose piece of tile. "She's a machine, that woman."

"Yes, she is," Meg agreed. "But you should probably check in on her later."

"I'll do that," Lindsay said.

Their eyes locked, and for a moment, neither of them said anything. Heat prickled at the back of Lindsay's neck, that unmistakable sense that something was shifting between them.

Meg cleared her throat and pushed her chair back. "I should get going. I have a tonne of paperwork to get through tonight."

Lindsay walked Meg to the door.

"Thanks," Meg said. "For today. I had fun."

"Me too," Lindsay replied. Her eyes flicked to Meg's lips, lightly pink from lipstick or lip balm. She chewed on the inside of her mouth.

"You still owe me a dinner date, McAllister," Meg said, her voice soft and low.

"I won't forget," Lindsay replied.

"I won't let you," Meg said, tugging playfully on the side of Lindsay's shirt. "I'll see you at breakfast." It wasn't a request, Lindsay noted, but an expectation.

"It's a date," Lindsay replied without thinking.

"I should think so," Meg said. She leaned in, her lips brushing Lindsay's cheek, the touch searing through her skin, leaving her breathless.

The elevator dinged, breaking the moment.

"Night, McAllister," Meg said, turning and walking away.

Lindsay pressed a hand to her cheek, wondering how she was supposed to sleep now. Especially with Meg in the room right next door.

Back in her room, she thought about the coaching offer Den had floated when she'd seen her back home. After a day spent having fun at the arcade, finding a genuine connection with Meg, and seeing the positive impact she'd had on Ellie, the idea didn't seem so crazy anymore. For the first time, she wasn't just thinking about how the money could help her business. She was thinking about the possibility of actually coaching.

SEVENTEEN

The next morning, Lindsay stepped into the dining room on a mission to find bacon, eggs and hash browns. After Meg's kiss last night, she'd hardly slept a wink and had woken up feeling hungover. A greasy breakfast would fix that, and she wasn't even worried about what Joey would say if he saw.

While she waited in the hot food line, she glanced around the dining room, finally spotting Meg at a corner table, the sunlight spilling across her hair. She was bent over a coffee and a colour-coded folder. Of course she'd be here early and working already. The sight of her made Lindsay's chest feel too tight and too full all at once. For a second, she was sixteen again, nerves fizzing in her veins, crushing on a girl for the first time.

As if sensing her, Meg lifted her head. Their eyes met, a slow smile blooming on Meg's face. Lindsay's heart skipped, and for a moment she was breathless.

What on earth was happening to her?

She shook herself and busied herself with piling bacon, eggs, toast and hashbrowns onto a plate, pouring herself a mug of coffee, and then winding her way across the room to Meg's table.

"Morning," Meg said as Lindsay slid into the seat across from her.

"Morning," Lindsay replied. She covered up her nerves by having a sip of her coffee. "What's on the agenda today?"

"Apart from a dinner date tonight?" Meg asked, playfully.

Lindsay's stomach did a little flip. Yes, she was definitely a teenager the way her body was reacting.

"If we don't get interrupted again," Lindsay said.

"Oh, we won't. I've cleared our schedules from five onwards," Meg replied, grinning.

Lindsay tucked in to her bacon and eggs. Meg continued.

"You've got a coaches meeting this morning while the team heads to the gym. Then…." Meg flipped a page over in her folder. "Set plays this afternoon, and then Joey's taking a cooking school tonight for the team."

"Oh, I'm bummed to be missing that," Lindsay joked.

"I doubt he'll be cooking steak," Meg teased.

"Who's cooking steak?" Den asked as she approached the table.

"We're wondering what Joey's cooking tonight," Meg said.

"Probably omelettes," Den replied with a tired smile. It looked like she'd had a hard night too. "Linds, can I see you when you're finished here? I'll be up in my room."

"Sure," Lindsay replied around a mouthful of scrambled eggs.

Den wandered away to the buffet.

Lindsay turned to Meg. "Do you know what that's about?"

"I do, but I can't tell you," Meg replied simply. She closed her folder and picked up her phone. "Should we choose where we're going tonight before we both get busy?"

"Sure," Lindsay replied. "I can't do omelettes."

Meg glanced up from her phone. "You're eating scrambled eggs."

"They're different," Lindsay said.

"Same principle," Meg said, shaking her head and looking back at her phone. She passed it to Lindsay, a list of restaurants on the screen. "Which one do you think?"

Lindsay scrolled the list. "That one," she said. Her fingers brushed Meg's when she handed the phone back, sending a fizz up her arm.

Meg lifted an eyebrow. "Lump-a-Rump?"

"You want steak, that sounds exactly like the place we need to go," Lindsay replied.

Meg scrolled on her phone, her cheeks dimpling as she smiled and nodded. "It's got four-and-a-half stars, so I guess it's a date."

They grinned at each other for what seemed like a stupidly long time until Meg's phone buzzed. She grimaced and slipped it into her bag. "I promise I will leave my phone in my room tonight."

"You better," Lindsay replied. "What time's dinner?"

"How about you pick me up at six?"

"Done," Lindsay nodded.

Meg hesitated, chewing on her bottom lip, and for a heartbeat Lindsay was sure they were both thinking the same thing - that she should lean across the table and kiss her. But then Meg stood up instead, a faint flush on her cheeks.

"See you at six," Meg said.

Lindsay watched her walk away, her breakfast suddenly forgotten. Maybe one of the perks of the job had nothing to do with soccer at all.

Den was on the phone when Lindsay entered her room. She indicated for Lindsay to sit on a chair at the table while she finished her call. It gave Lindsay time to check out Den's room.

It was bigger than Lindsay's, which was under-standable since Den was the head coach, and had a small round dining table with two tub chairs, one of which Lindsay was sitting on. Den was using the table as a desk, although the remnants of her breakfast were pushed to one side. She had a laptop open, and a small magnetic game board with round numbered magnets all over it. She was working on positioning the old school way.

Den finally finished her call and dropped into the tub chair across from Lindsay.

"Sorry, just finalising tomorrow's clinic," she said.

"I thought Meg did that stuff," Lindsay said.

Den shrugged a shoulder. "We hadn't finalised our involvement. I'll let Meg know when I see her."

"Are you sure that's wise?" Lindsay joked.

Den smiled a tired smile, and Lindsay got the feeling it was the first time she'd smiled since yesterday.

"How are you after the Gary… thing?" Lindsay asked.

Den raked her hand over her face. "It's always tough disciplining a staff member, but that's part of my job."

"I'm sorry I caused you problems," Lindsay said.

"It was going to happen at some point," Den said. She leaned back in her chair, relaxing just a little. "You're not the only one he's rubbed up the wrong way. He's been throwing his weight around for months. But it seems you standing up to him gave a couple of other people the confidence to speak up, and gave me enough evidence to do something about it."

Lindsay raised an eyebrow. "How does someone like that still have a job?"

Den huffed out a laugh. "Politics. The board thought he looked good on paper, so they turned a blind eye to everything else. I'm hoping they can't do that anymore, particularly now we have some support from the new owners."

"Figures," Lindsay said. "Men like him always fail upwards."

"Tell me about it," Den said. "Anyway, I didn't bring you here to talk about Gary. I wanted to tell you that I'm impressed with the impact you've had on Ellie already."

Lindsay shifted in her chair, uncomfortable with the compliment. "I just did what anyone else would have done."

"No," Den said holding Lindsay's gaze. "Most people wouldn't. You got exactly where Ellie's head was at yesterday and shifted her mindset. You've done more in a couple of days than Gary did in months."

Lindsay fidgeted with a seam on her track pants. "I just—"

"Just take the compliment, Linds," Den cut her off.

Lindsay huffed out a laugh. "Okay then. Thanks."

Den leaned in, her voice dropping into no-nonsense coach mode. "Obviously I can't say too much at the moment, but it looks like I'll be in the market for a new senior assistant coach soon."

Lindsay let the weight of those words sink in. "You're sacking him?"

"Not my call," Den said. "But the new team owners will be here tomorrow for the clinic. PR stuff, mostly, but they've been made aware that Gary's now had multiple warnings for his behaviour."

"Right…" Lindsay replied. "So they'll sack him?"

Den puffed out a breath. "That has been Meg's recommendation, yes."

Lindsay leaned back in her chair. "I just… wow."

"I know," Den said. "If that happens, I want to get that position filled as soon as I can."

"Good idea," Lindsay agreed. "I'm sure the transition will be easy with Mike or one of the other coaches."

"I'm offering it to you, Linds."

Lindsay froze. "No, you're not."

"Um, yeah, I am." Den pointed at herself. "Head coach, remember? I get to choose my own staff."

"I don't have any experience," Lindsay said.

"You get experience by doing, Linds," Den said. "This is me giving you the opportunity to get experience."

Lindsay stared at her. "Surely one of the other coaches deserve the job. They've been working their whole lives to get an opportunity like this."

"Actually, they all agree with me," Den said, a self-satisfied smile on her face. Her tone softened into friend mode. "Look, Linds. I don't know what's going on with your business and whether you even want this. But I think you'd make a phenomenal coach, and I'd like that to be with me."

Lindsay's head spun. A month ago, soccer wasn't even on her radar. Four days ago, she'd reluctantly agreed to help Den out, more for the money and time to clear her head than any real desire to be back around the game again. Now she had the opportunity to make it more permanent.

"Is this a permanent thing, or just for the tournament?"

"The tournament for now, with an option to extend," Den replied.

Lindsay blew out a long breath. "Can I think about it?"

"Of course," Den said. An alarm pinged on her phone. "We've got a meeting to get to."

They both stood, heading for the door.

"Do I need to get Meg to convince you?" Den asked, a knowing smile playing on her lips.

Lindsay almost tripped over her own feet. She forced out a laugh, but inside, her heart beat just a little quicker. The scary thing was, Meg probably could convince Lindsay to stay.

EIGHTEEN

The first part of the coaches meeting was about code of conduct, which Lindsay guessed was a required thing after disciplining a coach. Gary sat at the back of the room, scowling, but he never said a word. From what Lindsay could see, most of the other coaches and staff pretended like he wasn't in the room.

Den then confirmed the details of the clinic they were running the next day at the stadium for local junior players.

"We're looking at around fifty kids all up across three sessions," Den said. "We'll have local coaches available to assist, and our players will jump in and help out as much as we can. Let's not end up with any injuries this time." She glanced over at Mike.

He put his hands up. "My hamstring is still feeling that last clinic."

Everyone laughed. Mike leaned into Lindsay. "I'm lucky Den didn't ban me after last time."

Lindsay laughed but before she could find out more, Den then moved on to Joey, who explained his cooking school.

"Coaches are also required to attend," he said, making them groan. "This is as much about you modelling good nutrition as the players understanding it themselves."

After the meeting, Lindsay messaged Meg. '*Looks like our date is on hold. I have to go to Joey's cooking show.*'

Meg messaged back almost immediately. '*An omelette isn't the same as a steak, but I guess it can pass as a date.*'

Lindsay grinned. '*A date with thirty other people in the room?*'

'*If I get to see you eat an omelette, I'm happy to forgo my steak.*'

Lindsay grinned, shoved her phone in her pocket and headed up to her room to grab her backpack. She wanted to head to the gym with the players and hopefully have a chat with both Grace and Ellie together. If she was going to be a proper assistant coach, even temporarily, then they needed to know she was in their corner now.

Lindsay had planned to use the gym session to get some proper coach time with Ellie and Grace, and maybe start building a bit of trust. When they were setting up at the gym, Grace said, "You used to play with Olivia's aunt."

Lindsay blinked. So much for easing her way in. "Who's Olivia's aunt? And who is Olivia?"

"Rookie," Ellie said, nodding to where the two rookies who were fitted for their uniforms the same day as Lindsay were pulling off their club jackets.

"Her aunt is AJ Gill," Grace said. She pulled off her long-sleeve shirt and shoved it in her backpack. She sat on the ground with Ellie and started stretching.

Lindsay glanced back across at Olivia, who spotted her looking and smiled. Lindsay smiled back. "How do you know that?"

Grace rolled her eyes. "There's this thing called the internet."

"You Googled me?" Lindsay asked.

"Duh," Grace replied, barely concealing her eyeroll. "We Google all our coaches."

"And our team mates," Ellie added.

"Right," Lindsay said. She hadn't heard about AJ in years. "What else did the internet say about me and AJ?"

"AJ's coaching in Sydney," Ellie said. "But Olivia told us that."

"You were a goalkeeper too," Grace said. "Were you any good?"

The nerve of these kids, Lindsay thought. "Better than okay," she replied. "But I'll let you Google that."

Ellie laughed. "Ooh, sick burn."

"Shut up," Grace said, but with good humour.

"I didn't have all this stuff to help with training though," Lindsay said. "And I wasn't paid to play."

The girls looked at each other. "We're not paid that much," Ellie said. "Most of us have other jobs."

"Yeah, it's not like it's full time or anything," Grace said.

"It's better than nothing," Lindsay said. "Playing soccer cost me a lot of money, even when I made rep sides."

"Are you going to tell us to be grateful for what we have now?" Grace asked, barely containing her sass.

Lindsay laughed. "No. But I will tell you that you're probably still going to have to fight for everything you get, and that you should definitely never give up."

"Oh," Grace said.

"Exactly," Lindsay said. "Now stop yapping and show me what you've got."

"Yes, Coach," Grace said, doing a mock salute.

Ellie ducked her head to hide her smile, but Lindsay caught it. She could see what Gary was talking about with the differences between Ellie's and Grace's personalities. They might be chalk and cheese, but they both had something Lindsay could work with.

NINETEEN

AFTER THE SET PLAYS session, Lindsay had some business phone calls she needed to return, so by the time she got to the dining room, Joey was half-way through making his omelette.

He had two Mustangs players at the table with him, cooking alongside him, showing off for their team mates, their team mates playing along. She spotted Meg at a table at the back and wandered over and took the seat beside her.

"I thought you'd skipped out on our date," Meg whispered.

"Not a chance," Lindsay replied. "Do we get to taste test at this demonstration?"

"The girls will," Meg replied. "I'm hoping he's finished soon so we can still go and grab that steak."

Meg put her hand on Lindsay's, resting on her knee. Warmth spread through Lindsay's body like honey and it took all her strength not to levitate right off the chair. She was nervous, too, about what would be said if they got caught.

Finally, Joey and his assistants plated their omelettes and invited everyone up for a taste.

"That's our cue," Meg whispered.

She and Lindsay stood up and walked towards the door. Joey called them out. "You're not leaving before my protein pancakes?"

"We've got dessert covered somewhere else," Meg said, ushering Lindsay out the door. They almost crashed into Den, who was coming out of the lift.

"Where are you two off to?" she asked, eyebrow lifted.

"Lindsay needs red meat," Meg said, grabbing her arm. "Joey's making pancakes though."

"I love pancakes," Den replied. She paused, and Lindsay thought she was going to say something about her and Meg. Instead, she said with a knowing smile, "Don't stay out too late."

"We won't," Lindsay promised, letting Meg drag her away and out of the motel.

Lindsay didn't know whether Den not mentioning her burgeoning relationship with Meg was a good thing or a bad thing. Should a coach, even a temporary one, be dating the Ops Manager? Meg clearly didn't care, and if she wasn't worried, maybe Lindsay didn't need to be either.

They wandered down the street for a block before Lindsay said, "Do you know where you're going?"

"Sort of," Meg replied. "It's down this way. I just don't know how far."

"You don't want to use Google maps?" Lindsay teased.

"Let's fly by the seat of our pants and see where we end up," Meg said with a wink. She hooked her arm into Lindsay's, and they wandered down the paved main street in companionable silence, stopping and looking in at shop windows every now and then. Lindsay was hyper-aware of every brush of Meg's sleeve on her arm, the closeness when they leaned into the same shop window, faces close enough to arc against each other.

It took all Lindsay's strength to keep her breath and heart steady.

When they finally arrived at Lump-a-Rump, Lindsay said, "You knew exactly where we were going."

Meg opened the door and indicated for Lindsay to go in first. "Of course I did. I always know where I'm going."

They were seated in a booth at the back, close to the kitchen so they could see other people's orders being brought out. Meg watched eagle-eyed at everything, deciding what she'd order. Despite the name, the Lump-a-Rump also served food other than steak and even had a few vegetarian options.

By the time a waiter brought their drinks and took their order, Lindsay knew exactly what she'd order – the 500g rump steak, medium, and vegetables. She was surprised and a little impressed when Meg ordered the same.

"I told you I'm a steak girl," Meg said.

Lindsay's chest tightened, and she found herself staring at her beer instead of at Meg's eyes. Why was she nervous all of a sudden?

Meg, as she had done for the last few days, pulled her back and knew exactly what to say. "So, this is where we're supposed to do small talk."

Lindsay snorted. "I guess it is."

"You go first," Meg said. "Ask me your most burning question."

Lindsay thought about it for a moment, and finally asked, "Why an ops manager with a women's soccer team?"

"Ooh, good question, McAllister," Meg replied. She sipped her wine and did a thing with her mouth that made Lindsay want to kiss her. "This is going to sound corny, and a little feminist, but I wanted to work somewhere I could make a difference to women. I worked corporate, and it's such a swinging dicks club, I couldn't stand it."

Lindsay laughed out loud at the swinging dicks comment. "Soccer is still like that you know."

Meg nodded. "I know. But at least I get to kick some of them in the shins occasionally."

Lindsay laughed.

Meg continued. "The Mustangs have just been bought by a group of women investors, did you know that?"

"I did not," Lindsay admitted. Maybe she needed to do some Googling herself.

"The deal was rubber stamped a month ago." Meg leaned back in her chair, twisting her wine glass in her hands. "You'll get to meet them tomorrow at the clinic."

Lindsay arched a brow. "I'll bet Den's happy about that."

"Oh, she's thrilled," Meg said with a smirk. "Gary? Not so much."

"Not a fan of someone looking over his shoulder?" Lindsay asked.

"Not a fan of being owned by women," Meg replied. "He'll play nice while he has to, but to be totally honest, we're just waiting for him to jump ship." She took a sip of her wine, her eyes narrowing slightly. "There are some big changes coming, and not everyone's going to like them. I'm excited though."

Lindsay arched a brow. "Gary's one of them, I'm guessing. Probably waiting for the team to win something substantial to pad his resume."

"Everyone does in this industry," Meg said. "You didn't though. You walked away at your peak from what I've heard and read."

"Ouch. Right to the heart," Lindsay said, only half joking.

Meg's face fell. "Oh, I didn't realise it was, like, a thing," she apologised. "The way Den talks about you and soccer, you just sort of fell away from it."

Lindsay took a breath and let it out. Then she took a long drink of her beer and decided that she wasn't going to mince her words, not with Meg.

"I had a terrible coach," she said bluntly.

"Like Gary," Meg said.

"Worse than Gary," Lindsay said. The memories of her early twenties trying to make it in elite soccer came flooding back. "He made the game feel like punishment. It was elite sport at its worst," she said quietly.

Meg covered Lindsay's hand in hers. "I'm so sorry that happened to you."

"Thank you," Lindsay said.

"No wonder you didn't want to come anywhere near it again."

"Well, all that's changed, apparently," Lindsay said with a small smile.

"Are you saying you're enjoying it again, McAllister?" Meg asked.

"I'm saying I'm not exactly hating being back around it," Lindsay admitted.

The weight of their conversation lifted when the waiter returned with their meals, setting down two massive plates of steak and vegetables. Lindsay said, "Finally, something I know how to tackle."

"I can't wait to see you get through that," Meg teased.

"Challenge accepted," Lindsay grinned.

Later, as they arrived at Meg's door, Lindsay felt more relaxed than she had in a long time. Talking with Meg over dinner had been easy, and opening up about her playing days had lifted a weight off her shoulders she hadn't realised she was carrying.

"So," Meg said, softly. "This is the part where we say goodnight."

"Supposedly," Lindsay replied, not taking her eyes off of Meg's. They were intoxicatingly blue, with green flecks. She swallowed hard, her pulse thudding in her ears.

Meg tilted her head, just enough for Lindsay to get the hint. Before she could lose her nerve, she leaned in. Their kiss was quick and soft, but it sent a rush of fire down her spine to her toes. When she pulled back, Meg's smile was slow, lazy.

"Better than protein pancakes," Meg said quietly.

"Much better," Lindsay agreed with a grin.

Meg stepped inside her room, eyes locked on Lindsay's. "Night, McAllister."

"Night, Meg." Lindsay waited until Meg's door closed and turned and floated down the hall to her room.

Lindsay threw herself on the bed fully clothed, unable to wipe the stupid grin off her face. For the first time in a long time, something other than soccer was making her heart race.

TWENTY

The next morning, Lindsay was still buzzing from the night before, and her breakfast with Meg had become charged with conspiratorial grins and giggles, and foot-touching under the table. She felt like a teenager again with her first crush. Even Gary's sulking energy permeating through the restaurant as he huffed around couldn't bring her down.

When they got to the stadium for the junior clinic, Lindsay was almost glad that Meg would be with the owners and PR team, otherwise she'd never have been able to wipe the goofy grin off her face.

Out on the field, it was clear who the stars of the morning were. She couldn't decide who was more excited, the kids or the Mustangs players. This was clearly something they enjoyed doing. She hung back, content just to watch the morning's clinic. The

Mustangs coaches had arrived earlier and set up drills stations and fun activities, so the kids were ready and roaring to go. Gary, apparently, had been put on marker duty, which he obviously was not happy with, judging by his scowl.

After the initial introductions, the kids were split into groups, and Mustangs players were spread amongst them as helpers and participants. The kids raced around the activities, laughing and giggling. Lindsay kept an eye on Ellie and Grace, who looked like they were having fun, encouraging young players, high-fiving. She also kept an eye on Gary but noted that he was being shadowed by another coach and kept well away from the two goalkeepers.

As she scanned the field, she noticed a girl, maybe eight or nine, sitting to the side in a bib that was way too big for her. She was picking at the grass, and occasionally watching what was going on, but didn't get up to play. Lindsay wandered over and sat down.

"To cool for soccer drills?" Lindsay asked.

"I'm not good enough," the girl replied.

"Well, neither am I but they let me hang around anyway," Lindsay replied, deadpan.

The girl looked Lindsay up and down, clocking her uniform. "Are you a player?" she asked.

Lindsay almost hugged her for thinking she looked young enough to play. "I used to play," she replied. "Now I teach other people to play."

"You can't teach me how to play. Alistair said I look like an idiot when I kick the ball," the girl said. It cracked Lindsay's heart to hear someone so young say that about themselves. She looked at the kids playing and wondered which one was Alistair.

"I tell you what," she said eventually. "You help me not look like an idiot and I'll help you not look like an idiot, deal?"

The girl grinned. "Deal."

Lindsay grabbed a bib from Mike who gave her a quizzical look. She just shook her head at him, and he handed her the bib and shrugged.

As she tugged the bib over her head, a voice muttered just loud enough for Lindsay to hear, "Nothing like a washed-up keeper telling kids how it should be done."

She glanced over to where Gary was standing, holding coloured cones and smirking.

The girl didn't seem to have heard it, but Lindsay caught it. So did Mike, judging by the look he gave her. She stiffened but kept her expression neutral.

Same old garbage from the same old neanderthals, she thought.

"By the way," Lindsay said as she grabbed a ball from the pile. "Alistair sounds like an idiot himself." She looked Gary dead in the eye. "Don't listen to idiots."

The girl giggled.

"What are we doing, Coach?" she asked Mike as she fixed the girl's bib so it fit her better.

Mike pointed to the field. "We're taking turns at dribbling through coloured gates."

Lindsay watched for a moment as kids dribbled balls through coloured cones and then passed off to their partner who did the same thing with a different coloured cone 'gate'.

"Right. Got it." She looked down at her partner. "I'm Coach Lindsay, by the way," she said, sticking out her hand.

The girl shook Lindsay's hand. "I'm Lucy."

"Right, Lucy, let's go show'em how it's done."

Lindsay dribbled the ball and guided Lucy onto the field and started walking through the drill. After a few goes at it, Lucy started to get the hang of it, and they both laughed and giggled their way around the field until Mike blew the whistle to stop and move to the next one.

Lindsay started to pull her bib off as she walked Lucy to Den's station. Lucy grabbed Lindsay's hand. "Can you help me again?"

Lindsay hesitated.

"Looks like you've found yourself a friend," Den said, grinning.

"Sure," Lindsay said to Lucy, pulling her bib back on. "Let's go." She glanced over to where Meg was standing with the PR team and photographers. She was smiling that melt-your-heart smile directly at Lindsay, and it took all of her strength to look away and concentrate on the drill.

Lindsay partnered Lucy through two more drills before she pulled Ellie aside and asked her to take Lucy under her wing for the rest of the session. She watched as the two of them laughed and joked, Lucy growing in confidence as the session wore on. Ellie encouraged and slowed things down to explain, and high-fived Lucy when she got things right. This was the type of leadership Ellie could give to the backline and the team.

She scanned the drills for Grace, and found her tearing around a small field, kids chasing after her, trying to grab a bib from the waistband of her shorts. She taunted them good-naturedly and when someone finally caught her, she fell to the ground. She popped up again, laughing, and grabbing the boy who'd tagged her on the shoulders and roughing up his hair.

The two goalkeepers were so different, but seeing them both have fun in their own way made Lindsay understand what both of them had been missing. What she'd been missing. Fun. Isn't that what Pop had told her? It was just a game. It was meant to be fun. That's what today was all about. Reminding these girls who were now getting paid to play that it was still supposed to be fun.

Finally, it was time for a drink before the final activity, where the kids got a chance to have shots at Ellie and Grace in goal.

"I'm gonna score," Lucy said with gusto as she drank from a plastic cup.

"I'm sure you will," Lindsay replied.

"You have to get past me," Ellie joked.

"You're a goalkeeper?" Lucy asked, her eyes wide.

"Yep," Ellie said. She glanced at Lindsay who just smiled knowingly. "So's Coach Lindsay."

"Really?"

"I was," Lindsay said. Without thinking she added, "But now I'm a coach of goalkeepers."

"That's so cool," Lucy said, obviously impressed. "I want to be a striker."

"Then we have to be sworn, mortal enemies," Ellie joked. She walked away with Lucy, chattering away about goalkeeping and striking.

Lindsay glanced around at the gaggle of Mustangs players and kids, all in small groups, laughing and talking. This, right here, was what she'd loved about the game. Why couldn't it always be like this?

Meg came to stand beside her, a little too close to be accidental. "You looked like you had fun."

"You know what? I actually did," Lindsay admitted. "Kids put the game in perspective."

Meg turned and looked at the groups of players having snacks and drinks. She leaned into Lindsay so their sides touched. Lindsay tried not to combust. "They do, don't they?"

A few minutes later, Den clapped her hands to get everyone's attention. "Okay, who wants to see if they can score a goal against our goalkeepers?"

Every kid's hand shot up, and so did the Mustangs players. Ellie pulled Grace's hand down, and they both laughed. Den led everyone, including the club owners, over to the goal where Ellie and Grace started putting on their gloves. As they were getting ready, Den threw Lindsay under the bus.

"While Ellie and Grace get ready, Coach Lindsay is going to tell you the number one rule of goalkeeping."

Behind her, Gary snorted, loud enough for the other coaches and the owners to hear.

"Number one rule is not to quit," he mumbled.

A couple of the PR staff exchanged looks. Den's jaw tightened but she didn't step in. The kids seemed oblivious to Gary's snark. The words hit harder than Lindsay wanted to admit, though. For a moment, she almost stepped back. Almost let him win. But then she felt Lucy's eyes on her, expectant, trusting.

And Meg, an eyebrow arched, clearly wanting to know the answer to Den's impromptu question.

"The number one rule of goalkeeping," Lindsay said. "Is…" She paused to stall and give herself time to think, but she hoped it made it look like what she'd say next was profound. Finally, she said, "to not get hit in the face."

The kids all burst out laughing, and Meg shook her head and grinned. And just like that, Gary's jab had lost its teeth.

Then Den really threw Lindsay under the bus. "Okay, our striker Jordan is going to show you how to have a shot from the penalty spot. And Coach Lindsay is going to show you how to not get hit in the face."

Lindsay narrowed her eyes and shot a glare at Den, but there was no way she could back out. Especially when she saw Lucy clapping and grinning. She let out a long breath as she walked over to Grace and Ellie. "Have you got any spare gloves?"

Grace grinned and handed her a pair of her training gloves. "Lucky I have small hands," Lindsay grumbled as Grace and Ellie helped her pull the gloves on.

"Let's see what *you've* got, Coach," Ellie said as she stepped away from the goal.

Lindsay walked over and set herself in the box. She tapped the crossbar above her, did a couple of jumps and over-emphasised stretches, making the kids laugh. If this was Den's way of convincing her to coach permanently, then she was sadly mistaken.

She set herself on the goal line and looked at Jordan, who was setting up her shot. She took a couple of steps back and looked up at Lindsay. She very briefly motioned with her hand in front of her leg, pointing to her left, Linday's right. Having no reason not to trust her, Lindsay decided she'd go right. Jordan would either be bluffing or not, but whatever happened, Lindsay would make the attempted save look as good as she could. She focused on the ball, pushing Jordan and the kids and the Mustangs out of her mind.

Jordan took one step, two steps, and then the ball was in the air, arcing to Lindsay's right. Lindsay took a step forward and launched herself, full stretch to her right. The ball thumped off her glove, pinged against the post and shot out into the goal box.

Everyone cheered, and as Lindsay stood up and brushed herself off, Ellie was in front of her high-fiving her.

"That was awesome, Coach!"

The kids jumped up, calling 'me next!', the coaches trying to wrangle them into groups.

"I want to shoot against Coach Lindsay, too," kids shouted.

"Looks like you're the favourite," Grace said, without a hint of malice.

"Favourite or no favourite, you can go next. I won't be able to walk if I do any more."

Grace and Ellie laughed, and Lindsay watched as they over-emphasised letting goals in or diving saves, making the kids laugh and celebrate. One kid, on scoring against Ellie, threw his shirt over his head and did the aeroplane celebration, running around the goal box high-fiving everyone as if he'd won the world cup.

Later, as the Mustangs players signed autographs for the kids, and Lindsay helped the coaches pack up, she felt a tug on her shirt.

"Can I get your autograph too, Coach Lindsay?"

It was Lucy, holding out a poster of the Mustangs team, signatures all over the player's team photo. Lindsay took the poster and the pen from Lucy. "I'm not in this photo," she said, looking for a spot to sign.

"Why not?" Lucy asked.

"I'm new to the team," Lindsay replied. She signed in a blank space at the top of the poster.

"I'm new too," Lucy said.

"To soccer? Is this your first year?"

Lucy nodded.

"Well, you looked like you'd been playing for at least ten years," Lindsay said.

Lucy giggled. "I'm only eight."

Lindsay handed back the poster and pen. "I thought you were at least fifteen the way you did those drills today."

Lucy's grin could have lit up the entire stadium. "Thanks! I have to get Ellie. Bye!"

Lindsay watched as Lucy ran off to talk to Ellie.

Meg stepped in beside her. "You're like the Pied Piper with kids."

Lindsay waved her away. "They don't know how grumpy soccer can make me."

"You? Grumpy? I don't believe it," Meg teased. They walked over to the group of kids, who were waving their goodbyes to the players and heading out the gates. Meg broke off to head to the publicity team.

"That was fun, huh?" Den said, crossing her arms.

"I guess so," Lindsay replied.

"You could have a whole lot more fun like that if you came on board permanently," Den teased.

"As long as you never throw me under the bus like that again," Lindsay replied.

"Oh, I don't know. I think you and I make a good team. The kids loved it."

"You loved it," Lindsay replied.

"Yeah," Den said, nodding her head. "I did love seeing you in the sticks again. I wasn't the only one, though."

Lindsay followed Den's gaze to the publicity team who were talking to Meg. As if she knew they were talking about her, Meg glanced up and smiled. In that moment, everything seemed to click into place. She'd spent the morning coaching and mentoring, and even playing. And for the first time in a long time, she'd loved it.

Pop's words echoed in her mind. *Soccer is a game, Lindsay. It's not meant to be serious.*

Today hadn't been serious. It had been fun. Signing Lucy's poster as 'Coach Lindsay' had felt as natural as breathing. Butterflies stirred in her stomach, catching her off guard. She hadn't felt them in years. Not for soccer, anyway.

Den shoved Lindsay with her shoulder. "Come on, Coach. It's tradition on the last night of camp for the coaches to go out to dinner and leave the team to their own devices to play up."

Lindsay waved at Meg, who waved back, and then she fell into step beside Den as they headed to the team bus. It hit her, then, that she was contemplating taking a coaching job with Den. She wondered what Pop would say.

TWENTY-ONE

THE fiRST THING LINDSAY did when she got back to
the motel was call Pop and tell him her news about
being offered a coaching spot if it became available.
He was ecstatic, but he was more excited hearing
about the clinic she'd been to with the kids.

"Kids put the game into perspective," he said, sage-
ly.

Lindsay rolled her eyes, but only because she knew
he couldn't see her. "I know. That's what I said to
Meg."

"Hmm," Pop said at the mention of Meg's name.

"What?" Lindsay asked.

"Your tone changed when you mentioned Meg.
I'm guessing everything is going well?"

Lindsay couldn't help the grin that had spread to
her face but she didn't want to get Pop too excited.

It had been a while, years in fact, since she'd had a girlfriend, or had even dated, for that matter.

"It's going okay, yeah."

"Good on you, Linds," Pop said. "It sounds like you've found your footing."

"You know what, I think I have," Lindsay admitted. She thought about Lucy, the kid from today, and the Mustangs players and how much they obviously loved the game and passed that on to the junior players. And she thought about Meg, who had been the friend in the team she'd needed, and now, maybe something more.

She'd been working on her own for so long, she'd forgotten what being part of a team felt like. And how much she'd missed it.

"I have to get going, Pop. I have a coaches dinner to get to."

"Enjoy yourself, Linds. And I'll see you tomorrow," Pop said, and hung up.

She tucked her phone into her pocket, grabbed her jacket from the chair and headed downstairs.

The coaches were settling in their seats at the Italian restaurant they'd chosen when Meg walked in. Gary was noticeably absent, and Lindsay wondered if he'd chosen to stay away or if his restricted duties meant social events were off-limits. No-one else seemed to notice, or if they did, no-one mentioned it, so Lindsay didn't either.

"You're not a coach," Lindsay said as Meg took the seat beside her.

"No, but I do wield the club credit card, so you will need me to pay for your dinner." Meg nudged Lindsay with her shoulder, sending a buzz down Lindsay's arm and into her chest.

There was general chatter as they ordered drinks and scanned the menu and once everyone had ordered, Den stood up and quieted the table.

"Just quickly, because I know we're all sick of soccer talk," she started, causing a ripple of laughter around the table. "Thank you for a successful week. Today's clinic was one of the best ones we've held and that's in no small part to your organisation and enthusiasm." She lifted her glass to her coaches.

"Also, quick announcement before I let you all take bets on what the team are up to without us, the PR team are planning an all-new campaign with 'don't get hit in the face' as the tagline."

The table erupted into laughter and good-natured jeers at Lindsay. Lindsay caught Meg's eye and was met with a quiet approving nod and smile. She felt Meg's hand squeeze her knee and almost combusted on the spot.

Garlic bread and entrees were delivered and talk turned to the team back at the motel.

"Did you sort the food out?" Den asked Joey.

He nodded. "I filled the fridge and pantry with every lolly and snack the players have ever mentioned. And there's ice-cream in the freezer."

"Good stuff," Den nodded.

Lindsay glanced at Den, questioning.

Joey said, "They can never, ever know it was me." He pointed at Lindsay, mock-seriousness on his face.

"Your secret is safe with me," Linsday replied, crossing her heart for emphasis.

"I wonder if Ellie will run her poker tournament?" Mike asked from the end of the table as he bit into a piece of garlic bread.

"Ellie?" Linday said.

"You think she's quiet and unassuming," Mike joked. "But she'll be running some sort of black market operations with Tim Tams by the time we get back."

The coaches laughed.

"Those rookies will have everyone learning dance moves for Tik Tok," Den said. "Olivia tried to show me one yesterday."

"They did one in the gym on Monday," Mike said. "They think I don't know, but they forget there are mirrors everywhere in there."

Lindsay got lost in the conversation and the fun ribbing of each other and the players that showed how much the coaches paid attention to them and how well they knew them. Along with Meg's occasional knee squeeze, Lindsay knew she'd made the right decision to help Den get through the camp.

At the end of the night, when the coaches had all gone back to their rooms, and the girls had quietly cleaned up whatever messes they'd made to try to hide their shenanigans, Meg and Lindsay found themselves lingering outside Meg's door again.

"Do you… want to come in?" Meg asked, one eyebrow quirked.

"Yes," Lindsay replied. "Yes, I do."

She let Meg take her hand and lead her into her room. It was as organised and neat and tidy as Lindsay expected. A suitcase was laying open on the chair, neatly packed, and a jacket hung on a hanger on the door to the wardrobe. Lindsay would bet Meg was the type of person to completely unpack and hang her clothes in the wardrobe and her underwear in the drawers. Unlike Lindsay who had lived out of her duffle bag for the week.

Meg drew Lindsay out onto the balcony in the cool night air and for a long moment they stood, hands intertwined, looking out over the park.

"Is this like the last night of summer camp," Lindsay teased, "where we promise to stay in touch, and then tomorrow we go our separate ways and never see each other again?"

Meg stepped closer, sliding an arm around Lindsay's waist until Lindsay instinctively wrapped her arm across Meg's shoulder. "Not likely, McAllister," she murmured. "Because I'm going to see you when you come and sign your coaching contract." Her fingers brushed Lindsay's side in a playful tickle.

Lindsay bit her lip, fighting back the sound rising in her throat.

"What coaching contract?"

"I know Den's offered it to you." Meg's eyes sparkled, amused, like she could see straight through Lindsay's protests.

"I haven't accepted it yet," Lindsay said. The words sounded flimsy the moment they left her mouth. "Besides, it's not available, is it?"

Meg tilted her face up, her voice low and certain, her eyes soft. "It's not yet, but when it is, you will." A heartbeat passed, and then her smile curved, mischievous and daring. "This is where you kiss me."

Lindsay didn't need to be asked twice. She leaned in slowly, hovering just close enough to feel the warmth of Meg's breath. She lingered, savouring the closeness and the possibility. Then she closed the distance.

The kiss began soft, tentative. But when Meg let out a quiet moan, Lindsay nearly unravelled. They shifted to face each other, Lindsay's hands sliding into Meg's hair, Meg's palms pressing against Lindsay's back, pulling her in. The kiss deepened, hungrier, threaded with longing.

Finally Lindsay broke away, breathless, her forehead resting against Meg's. She swallowed hard, her chest rising and falling as if she'd just played a full match plus extra time.

"I really should go," Lindsay said. "I have an early bus to catch."

"Yeah, you should," Meg whispered. She didn't let Lindsay go, though, her arms tightening around Lindsay's waist.

Lindsay shook her head and leaned in. "You're not making this easy."

"Wasn't planning on it." Meg's husky reply told Lindsay all she needed to know about the promise of what could happen next, if she'd let it.

They stood there a moment longer, Lindsay's heart pounding, caught between wanting to stay and not wanting to move too fast. She kissed Meg again, slowly this time, memorising the curve of Meg's lips with her tongue.

When they finally eased apart, Meg's smile was smug, softened by the warmth in her eyes. "Goodnight, McAllister."

"Night," Lindsay said. She forced herself to step back, breaking the touch. Reluctantly, she turned and walked inside and through Meg's room, down the hall and into her own.

Lying in the dark, the taste of Meg still burning on her lips, Lindsay knew that sleep, and her heart, didn't stand a chance.

TWENTY-TWO

LINDSAY THOUGHT SHE'D BE alone in the dining room the next morning, considering how early it was, but there were players and a few coaches scattered around the tables. She was disappointed to not spot Meg, but maybe she was sleeping in. It was the first time Lindsay had beaten her down for breakfast. She'd have to remember to rib her about it when she saw her.

With no Joey in sight, Lindsay piled her plate high with bacon, eggs and french toast with maple syrup, and sat at hers and Meg's usual table by the window where she could see the street. She had just over an hour before she had to be at the station to catch the bus home and she was hoping to catch both Meg and Den before she left.

It was Den who joined her first, dropping into the seat across from her with a mug of coffee.

"Morning," she said, her smile not quite reaching her eyes.

"Morning," Lindsay replied. "Everything okay?"

"Gary was sent home last night," Den replied.

Lindsay blinked.

"What happened?"

Den let out a breath. "Gary tripped over his own feet is what happened."

"Okay…"

"The owners weren't just here for the PR yesterday, Linds," Den said. "I asked them to be there to see Gary for themselves."

"So, they sacked him? Just like that?" Lindsay asked.

"Suspended indefinitely," Den clarified. "So that coaching spot we talked about? It's officially available, and I want you in it."

"Are you sure?" Lindsay asked.

"Can you please stop asking me that?" Den said. "Do you want me to get down on one knee?"

Lindsay laughed. "No. That won't be necessary."

"Good," Den said. "Because if your knees are as bad as mine, you'll know I'll never be able to get back up."

Lindsay smiled into her coffee. She'd already made up her mind the moment she'd signed Lucy's poster as *Coach Lindsay*, and her decision was cemented last night at the coaches dinner, but Den didn't need to know that yet. Drawing this out was far too much fun.

"How long do I have to decide?" she asked, feigning indecision.

"A week. The first game is in two weeks and I'd like you to attend at least one training session before kick-off."

"I just don't know if I'm ready for something like this, Den."

"You're never ready for it, I can tell you that now," Den said. "But if you wait until you're ready, you'll never do anything."

It was hard to argue with motivational Den when she was in full swing. And pointless, since Lindsay was already on board.

"I don't have anywhere to stay," she said instead, stabbing at her bacon.

"Meg's got you sorted," Den replied with a smirk. "She mentioned in passing that her *guest* room is available and would save the club money on a motel for you."

Lindsay arched an eyebrow. "You two have already decided, then?"

Den shrugged. "Pretty much."

The thought of living under the same roof as Meg made her stomach flutter, but she kept her voice neutral. "Makes sense." She set her fork down, met Den's eyes and finally let her off the hook. "I'm in. For the tournament, at least."

Den's grin spread low and wide. "Knew you'd get there."

"Don't make me regret it," Lindsay said.

She glanced past Den to the doorway where Meg had just entered.

Den followed her gaze, and then leaned back in her chair, glancing back at Lindsay. "You two actually make a pretty cute couple," she said, smirking.

Lindsay rolled her eyes, hiding her grin with another bite of bacon.

"Just don't go breaking my Ops Manager's heart in the middle of a tournament," Den added.

"What makes you think she won't break mine?" Lindsay countered, teasing.

Den threw her head back and laughed. "Well that's unlikely. I'll leave you two to say goodbye to each other." She stood up, muttered 'Young love,' just loud enough for Lindsay to hear, and weaved her way through the tables to the buffet.

Lindsay tried to brush it off with a shake of her head, but when her eyes lifted and met Meg's across the room, the flutter in her chest made Den's words hard to ignore.

As Meg wove her way to their table, Lindsay realised that for the first time in a long time, the idea of what came next didn't terrify her. Not with Meg smiling at her like that.

By the time the team bus pulled away, full of chatter and waving hands, it was just Lindsay and Meg left on the footpath. Lindsay immediately noticed how quiet it was, just the two of them, with the team on their way back to Brisbane.

Meg broke the silence. "We better get you to the bus."

Lindsay hefted her duffle bag onto her shoulder and followed Meg to the car. She dumped her bag in the back seat and climbed into the passenger seat.

Neither of them said a word for the first few minutes until finally, Meg said, "I'll see you in two weeks." They were simple words, but Lindsay heard what they meant. That it would be a long fourteen days. Without thinking, Lindsay rested her hand on Meg's knee. Meg covered Lindsay's hand with her own, the light squeeze saying more than words could in that moment.

They stopped at a set of lights and Meg said, "So the spare room is yours, if you want it."

It was the first time Lindsay had heard Meg sound unsure of herself.

"If you're sure it won't be a hassle," Lindsay replied. "I don't want to be in your way."

The lights changed to green, and Meg drove forward. "Well, it just makes sense. I'm only a couple of blocks from the stadium, and it will save us some money in the budget. And you don't have to find somewhere yourself."

"The budget. Right," Lindsay said, trying to hide a smirk.

Meg was waffling, Lindsay realised. Which meant she was nervous. She decided to put her out of her misery.

"As long as it won't put you out," Lindsay said.

"It's practical. And..." Her tone softened. "I want you there."

Lindsay's chest tightened. She turned to look out the window, watching the shop fronts fly by. There was no question she wanted to stay with Meg, to see where things would lead. She just didn't want to go too fast, too soon, and this... whatever this was with Meg... felt like a whirlwind already.

When they arrived at the bus station, they both sat in silence in the car, neither of them wanting to be the first to move. Then Lindsay leaned over and kissed Meg softly but with all the feeling she couldn't quite put into words. She rested her forehead on Meg's and whispered, "That should last us until we see each other again."

Meg pecked Lindsay on the lips. "A top up, just in case."

Lindsay got out of the car and grabbed her bag from the back. Meg laced her fingers through Lindsay's as they walked into the bus station.

"It's just two weeks," Lindsay said, as if reminding them both.

"I know," Meg said with a smile, tugging on the front of Lindsay's shirt.

The PA announced Lindsay's bus was boarding. "That's me," Lindsay said.

Meg leaned in and kissed Lindsay on the cheek. "Safe trip," she said.

"You too," Lindsay replied. She turned and walked through the automatic doors to her bus and shoved her bag in the compartment underneath. As she lined up to board, she turned, and seeing Meg still standing there, waved. Meg waved back, and then turned and walked away, and Lindsay climbed the stairs and found her seat.

In a few hours she'd be home with Pop, back to her old life to sort out her business. And for the first time in a long time, the thought of being back around a soccer team didn't terrify her.

TWENTY-THREE

After a week back home, Lindsay was climbing the walls. She'd tidied the front rose garden with Pop, she'd weeded the vegetable gardens, she'd replaced the crumbling sleepers in the back garden, and now, standing in front of the pantry in the kitchen, considering reorganising it, she realised she'd hit the wall. Alphabetising the spice rack? That was a new low. She closed the door with a groan.

Pop walked in, newspaper under one arm. "What's wrong with you?"

"I think I miss being ordered around by Den."

Pop chuckled. "You've got the bug again."

Lindsay shook her head. "I just… don't know what to do without the business."

"You could clean the shed for me," Pop teased.

Lindsay pulled a face. "I'm not that desperate."

Pop dropped into a chair at the kitchen table, spread the newspaper in front of him and hummed.

"What?" Lindsay asked.

"I reckon you already know what I'm about to say."

"Tell me anyway," Lindsay said, sliding into a chair across from him.

Pop took off his glasses and folded his arms across the paper. "Your head's in Brisbane already."

"That's not true," Lindsay said.

Pop smiled that all knowing smile that Lindsay both hated and loved. He was about to drop some wisdom she didn't want to hear, and he was probably going to be right.

"You rediscovered what it's like being around a team again," Pop said. "And you have Den… and a certain someone else to thank for that." His eyebrow arched, the corner of his mouth twitching.

Heat crept up Lindsay's neck. As if on cue, her phone buzzed. She picked it up to see a meme of a goalkeeper getting hit in the face with the ball, captioned *'She forgot the first rule'*. Lindsay bit back a laugh, but the grin spread across her face anyway.

"See?" Pop said, smug as ever. "That look. You've had it all week. Whenever your phone buzzes. I know that look, Linds."

Lindsay rolled her eyes. "Okay, yes. I like Meg. A lot actually."

Pop slid his glasses back on and looked down at his paper, still smiling. "Glad you're finally admitting it. Now, when are you heading down to Brisbane?"

"Den said I don't have to be down there until Friday," Lindsay replied. She pushed her chair back and wandered back into the kitchen, standing by the bench. She wasn't sure why she couldn't sit still.

"Since when do you do as you're told?" Pop teased.

"All the time," Lindsay replied.

Pop scoffed. "If you're serious about this, you could head down early. Weren't you saying you need to get paperwork signed? And you could settle in before you need to be back with the team."

Lindsay wanted to argue, but he wasn't wrong. The idea of doing the paperwork and then jumping straight back in to match preparation sounded exhausting. She crossed her arms. "I don't want to look desperate."

Pop peered over his glasses. "Den asked you to coach, remember? And besides, wanting to do the job properly isn't desperate. It's smart."

Lindsay didn't answer right away. The truth was, it wasn't just about getting the contract sorted. If she went early, even just a day or two, she'd get more time outside of soccer with Meg. Time without the chaos of camp or the structure and noise of match week.

Her chest swelled at the thought. "I'll think about it," she said, grabbing her phone off the table. "I don't even know whether Meg will be ready yet."

She messaged Meg. *Thinking of coming down early. Would that be okay with you?*

Meg's answer was quick. *Perfect. Can't wait :)*

Pop hummed again. "Your smile means you've already decided."

Lindsay rolled her eyes, but the grin tugging at her mouth gave her away.

TWENTY-FOUR

Lindsay followed the voice of her maps app through the western suburbs to Meg's apartment block. It stood, shiny and gleaming, fifteen stories high in a newer suburb where the streets still looked too clean, the trees were too perfectly trimmed and the cafes all had 'artisan' or 'collective' in them. It was worlds away from Pop's weatherboard house and veggie patch.

She parked in a visitor bay and craned her neck up at the glass and steel tower. It had that 'bought off-the-plan' developer look about it, but knowing Meg lived there eased Lindsay's misgivings.

Duffle bag slung over her shoulder, Lindsay walked through the automatic doors and across the marble-floored lobby, feeling out of place in her worn jeans and work boots. She half-expected someone to stop her, ask why she was there, but no-one did.

The lift pinged open and Lindsay stepped in, stabbing the tenth floor button. She caught sight of her reflection in the mirrored walls and chastised herself for not getting her hair cut before she'd left home.

When she knocked on Meg's door, it swung open almost immediately, as if Meg had been waiting on the other side. Barefoot, hair pulled into a loose bun, she looked like a softer version of the Meg that Lindsay had come to know at camp.

"Hey," Meg said, smiling, and the tension in Lindsay's neck melted.

"Hey," Lindsay echoed.

They hesitated for a moment before Meg stepped forward and hugged her. Lindsay sank into it, warm and solid, then too quickly it was gone.

"Sorry about the mess," Meg said, ushering Lindsay in. "I didn't get a chance to do a proper clean before you got here."

Lindsay glanced around as she followed her down the hall. It was anything but messy, but it was more homely than Lindsay had guessed it would be. It smelled faintly of coffee, the expensive barista kind, and something lightly flowery. Lavendar, maybe.

Rugs softened the tile floors, and a worn leather lounge faced shelves crowded with books and framed photos. It was warm, and lived-in.

"This is you," Meg said, pushing a door open. "It's not the biggest spare room, but I hope it's okay, for now."

The 'for now' caught Lindsay a little off-guard. Was Meg planning on Lindsay finding her own place at some point, or did she mean something else entirely?

Lindsay stepped inside and dropped her duffle bag at the foot of the bed. The room was neat, almost stark. A contrast to the living areas. Lindsay wondered if Meg ever used it. A double bed took up most of the room, with a built-in wardrobe across from the window, and a small desk on the other wall.

Meg leaned on the door frame. "Is it okay?"

Lindsay smiled and nodded. "It's great. Thanks."

"I don't use the wardrobe, so the space is all yours," Meg said. She stepped into the room and slid the door open. "I went and bought some new hangers. I didn't know what you'd need."

Lindsay stepped across and closed the space between them. "Meg…"

Meg turned.

Lindsay cupped Meg's face and kissed her. Lindsay felt Meg's smile against her lips. She'd been waiting too long for this moment and it didn't disappoint.

"Hi," Lindsay said when they broke apart.

"Hi," Meg replied, grinning. She pressed a hand to Lindsay's chest. "Are you hungry?"

"Starving."

"Good." Meg laced her fingers into Lindsay's and tugged her into the kitchen. "I made pasta."

Later, snuggled on the lounge together, the television on in the background, Meg slipped into Ops Manager mode. She laid out the plans for Lindsay's stadium tour the next day, ticking off the change rooms, gym, offices and boardroom.

Lindsay chuckled. "You know you get this little wrinkle right here—" she reached to brush her thumb between Meg's eyebrows "— when you go all Ops Manager Meg. It's very professional. And kinda cute."

Meg swatted her hand away, her cheeks flushed. "Go to bed before I put you on the tour schedule too."

"Does it come with a gift bag?" Lindsay teased, but she knew Meg was right. She needed some sleep. The next few days would be intense. Starting with the Mustangs as a coach, getting to know her way around the stadium and training pitches, and preparing for the first game in the Champions League.

They both stood and stretched and moved down the hall side-by-side. At Lindsay's door, Meg hesitated, her hand brushing against Lindsay's before dropping to her side.

"Sleep well," she said, her voice soft.

"You too," Lindsay replied.

Neither of them moved at first. Finally, Lindsay leaned against her door frame, smiling. "Thanks for letting me stay."

Meg shook her head and smiled. "I just... it made sense. Having you here."

Lindsay lingered before finally opening her door. "Night, Meg."

"Night, McAllister."

Lindsay watched as Meg padded down the hall, turning back at her doorway to smile before she disappeared inside.

Alone, Lindsay stretched out on the bed, staring up at the ceiling. Tomorrow, she'd step into a world she never thought she'd be in again.

The first time she'd gone in full of raw hope and ambition and it had burned her. The thought of going back made her chest tight.

But she wasn't twenty anymore, and she wasn't going in blind. Den was there again, but this time, she was calling the shots. And Meg, who made the idea of starting over feel like less of a risk and more like a second chance.

For the first time in years, Lindsay didn't just wonder if she could belong in soccer again. She wanted to.

TWENTY-FIVE

It was the first time Lindsay had seen a proper, new, built-for-purpose boutique soccer stadium, and the Mustangs home grounds, Akers Park, was something to behold. It was built to emulate the English non-league team stadiums with wrap-around stands, and the crowd close to the action on the pitch. It had a capacity of five thousand spectators, and Lindsay could only imagine what it was like to play in front of that many people. Last time she'd played, her team would have been lucky to attract a hundred people and most of them were just wandering through the park nearby.

There was a smaller pitch outside the stadium, surrounded by high fencing, specifically for training, and an enclosed artificial pitch to train on if the training pitch was too wet. She knew all of this from what Meg had told her, but pulling up in the staff car park and seeing it up close was something else. It was so much more than Lindsay had ever seen or experienced, it was hard not to be excited about how far women's soccer had come. This was what investing in women's soccer looked like.

She slung her bag over her shoulder and followed Meg into the administration building. The office was bigger than Lindsay had imagined. Who knew a soccer club would need so many people running around in the background?

Meg greeted almost everyone they passed, with a nod or question about their weekend or family. People straightened when they saw her, and Lindsay fell half a step behind, watching Meg in her element. It was clear she was well-respected here, and in charge.

By the time they reached the players' entrance, Meg was pulled aside by someone with a clipboard.

"Two minutes?" she said to Lindsay, shifting into problem-solving mode.

Lindsay wandered through the tunnel and up into the stands. She climbed until she was nearly at the back row and sank into one of the navy-blue seats. Pop would love the view from up here. She could see the entire pitch spread wide, impossibly green, the stands as close to the action as Lindsay had seen.

Groundskeepers were buzzing around the perimeter, erecting signage, ready for the weekend's opening game. Lindsay pulled out her phone, snapped a picture of the view and sent it to her Pop. Then she sent it to Meg. *Not a bad office you've got here.*

Meg's reply came almost instantly. *Best seat in the house. It'll be your office soon too.*

Lindsay smiled. *I hear the dugout is pretty exclusive. Do I need a lanyard to sit there?*

Meg replied *Cheeky. Behave McAllister. I'm on duty.*

Lindsay snorted. *I'm very professional. When does the tour start?*

You have to pay extra for that one.

Always a catch Lindsay sent back.

Meg replied *Perks of being in charge.*

Lindsay raised an eyebrow. *So you like being the boss?*

I am kind of a big deal around here Meg sent back, followed by a wink emoji.

Lindsay laughed. *Modest too.*

Don't roll your eyes at me, McAllister. People actually listen when I talk.

Lindsay smirked. *Maybe I'll take notes.*

You probably should Meg replied. *Someone has to keep you in line.*

Lindsay leaned back in her seat, shaking her head, grinning. *Good luck with that* she sent, imagining Meg's exasperated expression.

"You look happy to be here."

Lindsay jumped, glancing over the edge of the stand. Den's head popped around the wall below, eyes narrowed with suspicion but a grin tugging at her mouth.

"Just chilling out, waiting for the tour to start," Lindsay joked.

"They cost extra," Den said.

Lindsay laughed out loud. Was that a line everyone around here used? Den climbed the steps two at a time and dropped into the seat beside her. "Surveying your new domain?"

"It's pretty nice," Lindsay admitted.

"Purpose built," Den replied. "State-of-the-art everything. Cameras in every corner so we can pull game footage from any angle."

"Impressive," Lindsay said.

"Overkill," Den countered with a shrug. "I've always believed the dugout is where you can feel the rhythm of the game the best."

"You can see it best from up here," Lindsay said, glancing out over the empty pitch.

Den looked at her for a long moment. "Then sit up here. Pick your seat, I'll give you a mic and headset. I don't care if you're beside me on the bench or ten rows from the back. What matters is that you see what I can't."

Lindsay blinked. "You'd let me do that?"

"I brought you in for your eyes, Linds. Use them wherever they work best."

Lindsay leaned back again, staring out over the pitch. For the first time in years, someone was trusting her instincts. And that, more than the stadium, the cameras or the kit, made her chest ache in the best way possible.

Den slapped Lindsay's leg and stood up. "Come on. We've got work to do."

"Technically, I don't start until tomorrow when I sign my contract," Lindsay said, standing up.

"Technically, I don't care," Den replied. "Meg's finalising your paperwork anyway, so you may as well come and help me prep for Saturday."

Lindsay followed Den down the steps, nerves and anticipation tangling in her chest. Tomorrow, she'd officially be a Mustang, but today, she was already part of the team. And there was no turning back now.

Later that night, Meg was called back to work for an emergency board meeting.

"Everything okay?" Lindsay asked, as Meg shrugged on her jacket and grabbed her car keys from the tray beside the door.

"A late night board meeting is never a good sign," Meg said, as she kissed the top of Lindsay's head. "Don't wait up."

Lindsay tried to stay awake, but the quiet apartment and the low hum of the TV lulled her to sleep. The sound of the lock clicking open jolted her awake.

"Sorry," Meg whispered.

"S'okay," Lindsay mumbled, rubbing the sleep from her eyes and stretching. "What time is it?"

"Late," Meg said, her voice heavy with exhaustion. She shrugged off her jacket and hung it over the back of a chair. She kicked off her shoes and left them at the edge of the rug before she lowered herself onto the lounge beside Lindsay. She tucked herself against Lindsay's side, her head resting on Lindsay's shoulder like it was the most natural thing in the world.

Lindsay wrapped an arm around her, feeling Meg's body relax. "Want to talk about it?"

"Not tonight," Meg murmured. "Tomorrow."

Within minutes, Meg's breathing evened out, her weight sinking into Lindsay as she fell asleep.

Lindsay stayed perfectly still. She didn't want to move. Letting Meg lean on her - literally - felt strange and perfect all at once.

TWENTY-SIX

MEG HAD ALREADY BEEN in the office for two hours by the time Lindsay parked her ute in the staff car park the next morning. She'd gone into the office early, leaving a note along with a car pass on the kitchen counter for Lindsay when she woke up. Whatever Meg was dealing with must be important if she'd had to come in early after a late night last night.

She grabbed her backpack from the seat beside her and slung it over her shoulder as she strode across the asphalt to the admin building. She pulled the door open, greeting Bec and Jason at reception and winding her way through the cubicles, heading to Den's office.

Den was walking back up the hall when Lindsay ran into her.

"I was hoping you'd get here early," Den said. She turned Lindsay around and pulled her back the way she'd come and then took a left down the short hallway to Meg's office.

Meg looked up when they entered, her smile not quite the heart-melting one Lindsay was used to. Something was wrong.

"Hey," Lindsay said tentatively, glancing from Meg to Den.

"Hey," Meg replied. "We've hit a bit of a snag."

Lindsay's heart thumped. "What sort of a snag?" Her coaching credentials were up to date, and she'd completed all the necessary checks, Meg had made sure of that.

"Take a seat," Den said to Lindsay, indicating the chair beside hers.

"What's going on?" Lindsay asked, dropping into the chair.

Den scratched at her temple. "Slight change of plans."

"You don't want me to coach now?"

"Oh no, we want you to coach," Den said quickly. "It's just that... we can't employ you as a coach."

"I'm not volunteering," Lindsay said, starting to rise from her chair. "If I don't have a job, then I'll go home and… sort out my business."

Meg shuffled papers, avoiding Lindsay's eyes. "There is… a work around. It's not ideal, but—"

"We need to sign you as a player," Den cut in.

The word hit Lindsay harder than she expected. She froze, half upright, hands gripping the arm rests. "I'm sorry, what?"

Den let out a breath. "The board decided not to pay Gary out of his contract."

I don't understand," Lindsay said, dropping back into her chair. "He broke code of conduct. His contract should have been torn up."

"I agree with you," Den said. "The board closed ranks."

"They're protecting him," Lindsay deadpanned.

"Technically, he's still a coach until his contract runs out," Den confirmed. "Although he is suspended."

"Which means the coaching position isn't available," Meg clarified.

"That's what you were dealing with last night," Lindsay replied.

Meg nodded.

"If it were up to me, he'd be gone already," Den said. "But the board made their call and my hands are tied."

"My hands are tied too, unfortunately," Meg added softly. "But we do have a spare spot on the playing roster, and that is in my hands."

Lindsay looked between Meg and Den, not believing what she was hearing. "You want me back on a playing roster?"

"We'd be signing you to a rookie contract," Meg said, as if that made it any better. "They're shorter term. It's long enough to wait out Gary's contract. After that, we'll be free to sign you up as a coach."

Lindsay shook her head, trying to process. "I haven't played in years. Anyone with half a brain will see I don't belong out there."

"You might have to train once or twice," Den admitted. "Just when the board or owners are here."

"So they don't cotton on to the fact that I'm not actually a rookie?"

"Exactly," Den replied.

Meg leaned forward, her voice gentle but firm. "I think you're fitter than you give yourself credit for."

"Half of them have never played soccer before," Den said. "So they wouldn't know what a fit player looks like."

"Gee, thanks," Lindsay said.

"You know what I mean," Den said with a laugh. Then she got serious. "Look, Linds, I need you to sit on the bench with me, and to do that you have to be a member of staff or a player. I can't sign you as a member of staff because the board won't free up any more funds for me right now. But I do have a rookie spot on the roster. Will you have to train sometimes? Sure. You'll be there anyway training Ellie and Grace. But playing? You won't even have to kit up on game day."

"It's a grey area," Meg admitted. "But it's one no-one can argue with."

Lindsay sat back, weighing it up. She'd made peace with coming back after so many years away, and even started to believe she could belong in soccer again. But signing on as a player? And a rookie, of all things? Then again, if it was just on paper, and if it meant she could do the coaching role, maybe she could handle it.

"Is there a big pay difference?" she asked carefully.

"A substantial drop, I'm afraid," Meg admitted. "But we'll put you through the next level of your coaching qualifications as well while you're here. You'll need that anyway. We can fast-track you while you're 'playing' with us." Meg air-quoted the word 'playing'.

"And you get extra kit," Den said with a shrug.

"I think you'd look great in our playing kit," Meg teased, apparently trying to lighten the moment.

Lindsay ignored the attempted flirt from Meg and focused on the facts. The pay cut from what she was expecting as a coach stung, but a steady income was better than hunting for small, odd jobs to try to keep her business intact back home.

"So I sign as a rookie, assist as usual, and only train as a player when the board are around?" Lindsay asked.

"Yes," Den confirmed.

"And this is the only way you can keep me around?" Lindsay's gaze locked on Meg.

"This is the only way," Meg replied, her voice leaving no room for doubt.

Lindsay let out a slow breath. She could almost see herself doing it, signing quietly, ignoring 'rookie' and 'player', keeping her head down and getting through the weeks until the coaching role opened up. It wasn't ideal, but it might be workable.

Den must have sensed Lindsay's reluctance. "Look, Linds, I understand why you wouldn't want to do this. And it's perfectly easy for us to sit here and say 'oh it's just a contract. No big deal.' I know that. But here's the thing." She turned so that she was facing directly at Lindsay. "I need you on my side, Linds. I would walk over hot coals if that's what it took to get you signed. If a rookie contract isn't it? Meg and I will find something else."

"Is there anything else?" Lindsay asked.

Meg opened her mouth and then closed it again. She shook her head. "I'd… have to have a look at other positions. But for what Den needs, and because she needs you right now?" She shrugged her shoulders. "This is it, I'm afraid."

"Ellie told me what you said to her in the tunnel at camp," Den said, her voice soft, speaking as a friend now, not a potential boss. "And I'm going to say that exact same thing to you right now. You have some of the best soccer instincts going around. And whether you're signed as a player or a coach is semantics. This team could do with a positive role model, and whether you like it or not, you're the one they need. What I need."

Lindsay looked from Meg to Den and back again. Finally, she let out a breath. "I'm probably going to regret this."

Meg beamed and slid the contract and a pen across the desk. Lindsay picked up the pen and hesitated, just for a second. She was really going to do this. Come back to soccer, officially. She signed the contract and slid it back to Meg.

Den clapped Lindsay on the knee. "Welcome to the team."

TWENTY- SEVEN

The change room was empty when Lindsay stepped inside. The air smelled faintly of Dencorub, and kit was strewn around on the ground and on chairs, the same pre-training mess in the change rooms as it was at camp. It was oddly comforting.

"Your spot's set up. I'll see you out there," Den said. She turned and left Lindsay alone with the hush of the room.

She padded across the carpeted floor to the far wall where a training kit hung in an open locker. Fixed above it in bold block letters was McALLIS-TER.

Her chest swelled, just a little. She touched the lettering with her fingertips. She knew this was only a ruse, a workaround to keep her around, but seeing her name above a locker stirred up feelings she hadn't expected. Pride, dread, belonging, all jumbled together.

She quickly changed into her training strip and folded her clothes neatly in her locker. Den had placed a brand new pair of socks on the chair.

"Looks good on you."

Lindsay spun around. Meg leaned against the door frame, arms folded, a knowing smile tugging at her mouth.

"Don't get used to it," Lindsay replied, trying to dampen the moment.

"How does it feel?" Meg asked.

Lindsay pulled at her training shirt and looked down at herself. "Weird." 'Wrong' was another word Lindsay thought, but didn't say.

Meg stepped forward until she was standing in front of Lindsay. She tugged at the waistband of Lindsay's training shorts. "Liam is impeccable with his ability to size people up. These are a good fit."

"Do they tuck their shirts in anymore?" Lindsay asked.

Meg laughed. "No, and nothing will mark you as an 'oldie' with this lot than tucking in your shirt."

Lindsay smiled. "Noted."

"Come on. You've got a training session to get to and I've got some schmoozing to do with the new owners," Meg said, hooking her arm into Lindsay's.

They exited the change room, Lindsay turning left to head to the field and Meg turning right to head back up to the admin building.

As she reached the end of the tunnel, a shadow stepped out from behind the concrete column.

John Wickham.

Lindsay froze at the sight of her old coach, her skin prickling.

"You finally got your name on a locker," he said. "Must be nice, failing up after all these years."

Lindsay's throat tightened. "What do you want?"

"Nothing." He shrugged. "Just curious about what you're doing here."

"That's none of your business," Lindsay snapped.

"Oh, I think it is. Perks of being on the Ethics Committee. When I want to see what's going on in a club, I don't need an invitation."

Lindsay's blood drained to her feet. The irony of him being on an Ethics Committee was not lost on her. She wondered if he was the reason she couldn't sign a coaching contract.

Wickham leaned in. "I guess the new owners are big on empowerment. Must be why they're collecting strays. But it's funny. I don't recall anything at the last board meeting about a new member of staff."

Lindsay's jaw clenched. He was obviously trying to intimidate her.

He smiled then, slow and smug. "Still, it's nice Denise brought you back. Especially since your career was cut short. Shame really. You could have been something, if you'd been stronger." He straightened his jacket, and turned and walked away.

Lindsay's chest tightened, and she fought hard to breathe. She turned and headed back down the tunnel, her chest tight.

Her shoes squeaked on the polished concrete as she ran down one corridor and then another, not caring where she ended up but needing space. Needing air.

She crashed through the door to the admin building, vaguely aware of people in offices as she rushed past.

"Linds?" Meg asked, her voice muffled by the thudding in Lindsay's head.

Lindsay swallowed hard, her mouth suddenly dry. "I... can't..."

She back-pedalled and then turned, searching for the exit. She found a door, reefed it open, and stumbled into the car park.

The warm air slapped her in the face as she leaned over, hands braced on her knees, dragging in deep breaths.

"You're fast enough to be a winger."

Lindsay whipped her head around. Meg stood a few steps away, her arms hugged tight around her.

"Are you okay?"

Lindsay shook her head.

Meg stepped closer. "What's going on?"

"I can't…" Lindsay shook her head. "He's here."

Meg took another step forward and placed her hands on Lindsay's arms. The warmth of it steadied her. "Who's here?"

"My old coach," Lindsay replied.

Meg's face hardened and her tone got serious. "Which one?"

"Wickham," Lindsay mumbled. "John… Wickham."

"Okay," Meg nodded. "Okay. Well… that's going to be a tough one."

Lindsay glanced up.

Meg pulled a face. "He's… untouchable. He's an advisor on the Ethics Committee, which effectively gives him a free ticket to any club he wants."

"He told me," Lindsay said.

"You ran into him?" Meg's brows pinched together, the professional calm in her tone slipping.

"In the tunnel," Lindsay said. "On the way to training."

"What did he say to you?" Her eyes searched Lindsay's.

Lindsay shook her head. "He just reminded me of the truth."

Meg's hands tightened just a little on her arms. "Linds, I know how hard this is for you. And if I could kick him out of the club, I would. But this—" she glanced back toward the door, then back at Lindsay. "The fact that you're here, and you're doing this proves he didn't break you. You're not that kid anymore, Linds. You're someone the players are already looking up to. Someone Den trusts. And… someone I don't want to see walk away again. Not from the game, not from yourself. I… couldn't stand watching that."

She leaned in, close enough that if it were any other moment, Lindsay would kiss her. For a moment, she thought Meg might just do that. Instead, her voice dropped to a whisper. "You don't have to prove anything to him, Linds. Just show up for you. That's enough."

Lindsay drew in a long breath and slowly let it out. "It took me a long time to get over it, Meg. I've spent years building a life that had nothing to do with soccer. Now I'm supposed to just… pretend like none of that mattered?"

"It did matter," Meg said. "That's why it affects you so much. And it's why you're ready now."

Lindsay looked away, jaw tight, fighting against her instincts to flee again. She thought about camp. About Lucy's grin when she nailed a drill, Grace running wild with the kids chasing after her, Ellie shining in the squad game under the glare of so much pressure to perform. All of the things she'd missed about the game. All of the things she'd thought Wickham had beaten out of her.

Maybe it *was* time to prove to him, and to herself, that he didn't break her. Maybe it *was* time to stop running. From soccer, from herself, from everything.

She lifted her head, determined. "Okay," she said finally.

"Okay?" Meg asked.

"But if anyone calls me 'rookie', I'm out."

TWENTY-EIGHT

Lindsay caught the end of the warm-up, and as the team stretched and the coaches set up their drills, Den called all the players in. "Righto. I just want to quickly welcome Assistant Coach Lindsay McAllister to the team. You'll remember her from her amazing display of goalkeeping at the junior clinic in Toowoomba."

There were some claps and whistles that Den tamped down. "We're excited to say that she's agreed to join us. Her main role will be to mentor Ellie and Grace over the course of the tournament, and she has specifically asked me to tell you that you couldn't get her back in goal for real if you paid her, which we are not."

The team broke into laughter. Even Lindsay laughed at Den's joke. Her gaze drifted to the sideline where the owners stood with their arms fold-ed, watching.

Lindsay scanned for Meg and found her stand-ing with a group of mostly men in business at-tire and club jackets. The jackets looked pristine, and Lindsay wondered if they ever wore them outside of official club business. Hovering in the background was Wickham, standing away from everyone else, his arms crossed, face unreadable, but his eyes fixed on her.

Lindsay's jaw tightened. If he thought she was just here for looks, then she'd show him, and the board, just how wrong they were. She grabbed a bag of balls and followed Ellie and Grace to the goal box. She worked her way through familiar warm-up drills with an assistant coach, giving Ellie and Grace tips and encouragement where they needed it, but mostly just getting through the work.

Then it was time for crosses and even though Lindsay knew she should take it easy, she needed to prove to everyone watching that her signing was legitimate. When it was her turn in the box, she put in just as much work as Ellie and Grace did.

When Ellie's cross came looping over, Lindsay launched herself, tipping the ball over the bar with a stretch that had both Ellie and Grace cheering.

Her landing jarred her shoulder and her lower back was starting to complain, but she pushed herself up with a grin that dared everyone watching to doubt her.

The drills rolled on and Lindsay pushed far harder than she should have, diving, blocking, one-on-one saves, until her body was screaming at her. By the end, when Den finally called time on the session, Lindsay felt the stiffness starting to settle in her back and shoulder. She high-fived Ellie and Grace for a good session, determined not to let them see how much she was hurting.

As she filed into the tunnel with the team, she caught sight of John lingering by the tunnel entrance, a faint smirk on his face. Her chest tightened, but she straightened her shoulders through the pain.

As she reached for the change room door, Meg pulled her aside. "You might want to jump straight into an ice bath. That was quite a performance out there."

"I couldn't let him think he was right."

Meg's eyes softened. "You don't have to prove anything to him anymore, you know that, right?"

Lindsay didn't answer.

Meg touched her arm. "I'll be in my office. Come and get me when you're ready to go."

Lindsay tried to nod, but her neck was hurting now too. When she reached the change room door, Den said, "I signed you for your eyes, Linds. Not your keeping abilities. Ice bath. Now."

Lindsay rolled her eyes but wasn't going to diss Den in front of the team. She glanced back up the tunnel, but Wickham was gone.

TWENTY-NINE

LINDSAY LIMPED THROUGH THE apartment door and all but collapsed against the wall. Meg kicked the door closed behind them, tossing her keys into the tray. "This is what you get for showing off. What were you trying to prove, McAllister?"

"That I could still move," Lindsay said, grimacing as she straightened. "This is your fault. And Den's."

Meg folded her arms. "What makes you think this is my fault?"

"You're the ones who insisted on signing me to a rookie contract. That's why I had to train today," Lindsay said.

"Oh, so Den and I made you throw yourself around like a twenty-year-old?" Meg said, eyebrow arched.

Lindsay winced as she made her way towards the lounge. "No, but there was no way I was going to let Wickham think I couldn't hack it."

"And now you can't walk," Meg chastised.

"Can you please stop chastising me like I'm a child and help me get down?" Lindsay asked.

Meg stepped closer, her voice softening. "Come on. Let's see if I can patch you up before you're completely immobile." She gestured down the hall. "My bedroom. You'll fit better on the king."

"Oh, so you get the king bed while I'm slumming it on a double?" Lindsay muttered, hobbling after her. "Ops managers really do get all the perks."

Meg tossed a glance over her shoulder. "You're welcome to renegotiate your contract."

Lindsay chuckled, then winced, one hand pressed to her lower back.

In Meg's room, the bed was already turned down, pale blue sheets and pillows perfectly arranged. Lindsay lowered herself onto the bed with a groan. "I'm starting to think I signed with the wrong room mate."

Meg shook her head, perching on the edge of the mattress. "Turn over."

Lindsay raised an eyebrow. "Bossy."

"You need me to be," Meg countered. "Come on, face down."

Lindsay rolled her eyes theatrically, making Meg laugh, and rolled onto her stomach. The mattress dipped as Meg straddled the back of her thighs, her hands settling warm against Lindsay's shoulders.

The first press of Meg's thumbs made Lindsay hiss through her teeth.

"Too much?" Meg asked quickly.

"Too good," Lindsay mumbled into the pillow.

Meg worked slowly, thumbs kneading knots along Lindsay's shoulders, then down into the muscles of her back.

"Honestly, McAllister. You try so hard to look like you don't care, and then you go and practically break yourself just to prove a point."

"You saw that, huh?"

"Everyone did. Including Wickham." Her tone darkened for a second. "He watched you the entire time."

Lindsay let out a low groan. "That's why I couldn't stop. He already thinks I'm a fraud. I didn't want to give him any more ammo."

Meg's hands stilled for a moment, then pressed firmly into Lindsay's shoulders again. "He doesn't get to decide who you are anymore. You do."

"Thanks Dr Phil."

Meg swatted at Lindsay's arm. "It doesn't matter. You stole the show. The PR team were having a field day taking shots of you in action."

Lindsay buried her face in the pillow. Her aches eased under Meg's hand, warmth spreading through her chest. "Careful, you'll give me a big head."

"You already have one."

"Harsh."

Meg laughed softly, leaning down so her hair brushed Lindsay's ear. "Relax, McAllister."

Lindsay closed her eyes, relaxing under Meg's hands. With every knead and stroke, the air became charged.

Finally, Lindsay turned her head slightly, her voice rough. "Meg?"

"Mm?"

"If this is how you treat your rookies, I think I can live with it."

Meg's laugh was quiet but her hands didn't stop. She bent closer, her lips almost brushing Lindsay's temple. "This has nothing to do with you being a rookie."

The air between them grew too thick to ignore. Lindsay shifted, ignoring the twinge in her back, and rolled to look up at Meg.

Meg's eyes flicked between Lindsay's lips and her gaze, and for a second, neither of them moved.

"You're supposed to be relaxing," Meg murmured, her voice husky, her hands still resting lightly on Lindsay's sides.

"I am," Lindsay said, one eyebrow arched. "Just… differently."

Meg huffed out a laugh, but it broke when Lindsay shifted again, wincing as she pushed herself up onto her elbows.

"You're impossible," Meg whispered, her face close enough for Lindsay to feel her breath.

Lindsay lifted her chin, and Meg leaned down, closing the space between them. The kiss was nothing like the soft, tentative pecks they'd had before. This was hungry, weeks of tension breaking open. Meg responded instantly, her fingers tangling in Lindsay's shirt, pulling her closer.

When they finally broke apart for air, both breathless, Lindsay rested her forehead against Meg's.

"You should know," she said, her voice low, "there's no way I'm going back to that double bed tonight."

THIRTY

Keeping Ellie and Grace on task at training was no mean feat after they spent the morning at a media shoot. They laughed and giggled through their session, joking about each others' poses and who was most likely to end up with their face on the side of a bus.

Rather than stop them from having fun, Lindsay had leaned into it, letting them goof off for some of the drills before reining them back when it came for game strategies.

She was grateful to finally be able to crash on Meg's lounge, stretched out, watching game footage.

Meg sat beside her, laptop open and perched on her knees, while Lindsay watched clips of tomorrow's opposition on the TV with the sound down.

She leaned forward, elbows on her knees, rewinding and replaying a clip for the fourth time.

"They're going to score that goal no matter how many times you watch it," Meg teased.

"Ellie's never faced a side like this," Lindsay said. "They press high, and they're fast on the counter. They'll eat her alive if she hesitates."

Meg set her laptop aside and scooted closer so their thighs were touching. "You've been watching the same clips over and over."

"Because I need to make sure she's prepared," Lindsay snapped. She paused the footage and blew out a breath. "She's only nineteen. This is the biggest stage she's ever played on. One bad clip on social media and suddenly she's the 'keeper who cracked under pressure. People don't forget that. I should know, and we didn't even have social media when I was playing."

Meg placed her hand on Lindsay's knee. "She has you to make sure that doesn't happen."

"I can't stop the shots for her," Lindsay said. "The Chargers are a division above us. That's a whole different level. It could be a disaster."

Meg took the TV controls from Lindsay and placed them down beside her. "Now, you listen to me, McAllister. Ellie trusts you. You've given her more confidence in the last week than anyone's given her before that. That's going to be the difference for her tomorrow."

Lindsay shook her head. "Trust doesn't stop the ball hitting the back of the net."

"No," Meg agreed. "But belief stops her from falling apart when it does."

Lindsay bit the inside of her lip. She hated how much this game was under her skin again.

Meg leaned in, her voice softer. "You've been where she is right now. You know what she needs before she knows it herself. That's why Den wanted you here."

Lindsay slumped back against the lounge, still restless, wired and tired from the day and being out of her own comfort zone.

"I just don't want her to go through what I did."

Meg squeezed Lindsay's knee. "Well lucky for her, she has a much better coach than you did."

Lindsay tipped her head back against the lounge and for a long while, she didn't say anything. Then, she cracked one eye open. "You're annoying when you're right, you know that?"

Meg shrugged. "I'll take that." She laced her fingers into Lindsay's. "Now can we please watch something other than game footage?"

Lindsay let her head fall sideways onto Meg's shoulder. Tomorrow could wait.

THIRTY-ONE

The car park was buzzing when Lindsay and Meg pulled in, club and stadium staff all making their way in before the game kicked off in a couple of hours. Meg parked in her designated spot and killed the engine. For a moment, they sat in the car in the relative quiet, Lindsay staring up at the Akers Park sign. It had been years since she'd felt that familiar churn in her stomach of match day nerves, adrenaline and just a little bit of excitement.

"You ready?" Meg asked, her voice even. Her hand lingered on the gear stick, like she was ready to take Lindsay anywhere but here if she just asked her to. But Lindsay knew now that she didn't want to be anywhere else but here.

"As I'll ever be," Lindsay muttered. She reached for her bag in the back seat and slung it over her shoulder.

Once they reached the admin building, Meg hesitated. "You're all good?"

Lindsay nodded. "I'll see you down there."

"Yes you will," Meg said, smiling, and disappeared into the admin building.

Lindsay blew out a breath and headed to the Player's Entrance. It felt strange walking in this way, but there were cameras everywhere, and she couldn't risk their ruse being uncovered now.

Fans shouted player's names, waving jerseys and other club merchandise, hoping for autographs as players walked down the roped-off path.

Inside, the change room was already a hive of noise, with music thumping out of someone's speaker, and players in various states of readiness. Ellie was taping her wrists talking a mile a minute, Grace had her headphones in, bopping away, oblivious to everyone around her. Lindsay placed her bag in her locker and sat in her chair, taking it all in. She didn't need to get changed. She wasn't going to be playing.

Den appeared in front of her. "Got a sec?"

Lindsay followed her out into the tunnel, out of earshot of the team.

"The board want Grace in the starting line-up," Den said bluntly.

Lindsay blinked. "Grace is good but—"

"Ellie's better. I know," Den said. A door opened down further, and Den waited for the official to walk past before she continued. "If Ellie wobbles today, the board will have me for breakfast. So I need you to keep her steady out there. Can you do that?"

Lindsay nodded. "Of course I can."

Den clapped Lindsay on the shoulder. "Good." She turned and headed into the change room. Lindsay lingered for a moment wondering why the board would poke their noses into team selection.

She went back into the change room and straight over to Ellie and Grace, and sat them both down and gave them a quick pep talk.

"They play wide," she said. "Make sure you're always scanning."

Ellie nodded, her legs bouncing, clearly nervous.

"Your wide mids should track them. If they don't, make them," Lindsay continued. She thought about camp, and how much damage Gary had done before she'd come along. There was still a lot of damage to undo, but she hoped Ellie could hold it together for the opening game. She deserved her spot. She just needed to own it. "Use your instincts. Play the game as it comes, okay?"

"Okay," Ellie said, nodding. She sucked in a breath and let it out. "I can totally do this."

"You can totally do this," Grace said, grabbing Ellie's shoulders.

Mike called them out for warm-ups, and as Lindsay walked out the door, Meg caught her arm and tugged her back, away from the players.

"Ready for your first official game, Coach?"

"Technically, I'm not a coach," Lindsay said.

"Technically you're not a player, either," Meg shot back.

"So I'm neither."

Meg frowned. "What's with you?"

Lindsay hesitated. She didn't want to bother Meg with the boardroom politics she'd been dragged into. So she shrugged. "Nothing. Just… a lot riding on today."

"Yeah, it is. But being here at all is a win for us," Meg said, smiling.

"Only losers say that," Lindsay deadpanned.

Meg narrowed her eyes and softened her tone. "Okay, McAllister. If you're going to help Ellie keep her head, you need to keep yours first."

That pulled a small smile out of Lindsay. "Yes, boss."

Meg rolled her eyes, leaned in, and kissed her cheek. "Better. Now go do your job. I'll see you after."

From the bench, Lindsay tracked every touch, every pass, every movement. She noted the breakaways and the players they were targeting, thinking of ways the back line could shut them down.

Ellie, though? Ellie was on fire. She was sharp off her line, taking full control of her back line and the goal box. She was brave, too, coming out quickly and diving at strikers' feet to snuff out attacks.

Twice in the first fifteen minutes she kept the Mustangs in the game with full-length diving saves.

The pressure mounted, and if Lindsay could feel it on the bench, she knew Ellie would be feeling it on the field. Wave after wave of attack started to wear down the Mustangs mid-fielders who spent more and more time defending than attacking.

Lindsay's jaw ached from clenching her teeth. If she were a coach, she could stand up and pace alongside Den, but on paper, she was a player, a back-up goalkeeper, so she had to keep her butt rooted to the chair or she'd risk a yellow card.

Through it all, Ellie held strong, but the pressure was starting to suffocate them. The Chargers were showing them why they were the number two-rated Premier League team in the state.

They scraped into half-time at nil-all, staying in the match by the skin of their teeth and some fantastic saves by Ellie. Their chances up front were few and far between, though, and that put more pressure on their defence.

At the break, Den focused on the positives — the nil-all scoreline and their grit and determination. She urged them to stay in the contest and take the game play-by-play.

Lindsay told Ellie to slow the play down whenever she got the chance. Her team was getting overrun, and they weren't going to be able to match the Chargers on fitness. "You need to give them a break when you can," Lindsay said. "And watch the high balls this half. The sun might get in your eyes out there as it goes down."

Lindsay watched them file back out onto the field, hoping they had another forty-five minutes in them.

The second half started like a bomb with the Chargers executing a near-perfect set play from the kick-off, foiled only by the Mustangs centre back, who executed a perfectly-timed block just as the Chargers striker took her shot.

The Chargers lifted to another gear, and the Mustangs repelled attack after attack until finally, a Chargers cross floated into the box right between the penalty spot and six-yard box. Ellie hesitated, possibly thinking her backs would get a head on it, but they didn't challenge for it. Instead, the Chargers striker was left alone to score an un-contested header. Ellie made a valiant attempted diving save but couldn't get anywhere near it.

The Mustangs had barely kicked off when the Chargers scored again, winding their way down the left flank, cutting back to the edge of the box and the mid-fielder, who had threatened the whole match, scored their second.

Ellie's shoulders dropped, and Lindsay wished she could fix it, but there was nothing she could do.

Late in the second half, after the Chargers scored their fourth goal, Lindsay's gaze swept the stands in frustration. She found him sitting a few rows behind the dugout. Wickham wasn't cheering or watching the game. His eyes were on the dugout. Watching her. As the final whistle blew, he caught her eye, a slow, satisfied smirk spreading across his face before he stood up and left.

It was like the air had been sucked out of the stadium as the players trudged off the field.

Den tried her best to get the team to look at the positives of the game, but it didn't matter what level of opposition you played against, a loss was a loss. And Lindsay knew Ellie was going to feel it the most. She pulled her aside for a quiet talk.

"I know you're going to watch footage of that match," Lindsay said. "And when you do, I want you to see those goals from a fan perspective."

"What do you mean?" Ellie asked.

"They were almost unstoppable. All of them. It's why they're in the National Premier League. They're a great team."

"Is this meant to make me feel better?" Ellie asked, unconvinced.

"No. It's meant to make you not feel worse," Lindsay said, a smile tugging the corner of her mouth.

Ellie gave a small smile and shook her head. "That was a hard game."

"Yeah it was," Lindsay said. "Not many people can say they kept a clean sheet against last year's golden boot winner."

Ellie snapped her head up. "What?"

"That number ten, Sonia Hughes? Won golden boot last year. There wasn't a keeper in the NPL she didn't score against. And you just kept her scoreless."

A slow smile spread across Ellie's face. She nodded. "That's… pretty good."

Lindsay laughed. "Pretty good? I'd say that's a cracking day out." She clapped Ellie on her shoulder. "You should probably get to recovery before Mike comes looking for you."

"I will," Ellie said. "Thanks."

Ellie headed off to the physio room, and Lindsay grabbed her bag, slung it over her shoulder, and headed off to find Meg. They had three days to prepare for the next match, but Lindsay didn't want to think about that right now. Right now, she wanted something greasy for dinner, and she knew it wouldn't take much convincing for Meg to go on a fast food run on the way home.

THIRTY-TWO

Later that night, after hours of game analysis, Lindsay was at Meg's flicking through channels on the television, waiting for Meg to get home from her book club. Her body was tired from the day, but her brain refused to switch off. The game had been as intense from the bench as she'd ever remembered from the field, but the adrenalin rush was different.

When she played, she could switch it on and off so she didn't get hyped up so much that it affected her game. From the bench, as the game ebbed and flowed, Lindsay rode every pass, every play, every shot. She could feel the exhaustion starting to settle into her limbs. She just wished her brain would slow down enough for her to sleep.

She stopped on a sports channel showing highlights of the tournament. She watched snippets of the other teams in their opening matches. Clean passes, clinical finishes. It was soccer at a level Lindsay dreamed of playing once.

Then the screen cut to a press conference. Wickham was behind the microphone and rather than change the channel, Lindsay forced herself to keep watching, her jaw tight.

He was asked about the Mustangs chances of beating Riverside, their next opponents. He tilted his head in that way men like him did when they were about to regale you with some apparently hard-won wisdom, and said, "The Mustangs have potential but you have to question the professionalism of the entire setup. When they're signing a forty-something-year-old rookie who hasn't played in nearly two decades? I mean, we all love fairytales in this game but it makes a mockery of the level of competition in the Champions League just when the women's game is trying to look legitimate. You can't just bring in an old friend on a sham contract and expect to compete at this level. The league is supposed to be about results and showing the best of the best, not backroom deals and feel-good stories."

Lindsay's blood ran cold. She muted the TV but his words echoed in her head. He'd just accused Den of signing her to a sham contract on national TV. Technically, he was right, but he had no context about her signing at all. And now the whole country thought Lindsay was a sham. A washed-up has-been. She'd been painted as a joke to the tournament.

She turned off the TV, dropped the remote on the lounge, and walked out onto the balcony. The breeze was cool outside, and Lindsay hugged herself, leaning her elbows on the railing. This wasn't meant to be her story. She wasn't meant to be a fairytale comeback. She wasn't even technically a coach. She was… nothing.

The sliding door opened behind her. "Thought I'd find you out here." Her arms slid around Lindsay's waist. Lindsay leaned back into the embrace.

"How was your book club?"

"Good," Meg mumbled against Lindsay' s back. "Debs didn't realise it was a romantasy. It was a bit too… spicy for her."

Lindsay smiled and squeezed Meg's arm.

"Everything okay?" Meg asked.

"Did you hear Wickham's comments?"

Meg nodded against Lindsay's back. "I heard on the way home."

"This will affect the team," Lindsay said, her voice soft. "If this is hanging over their heads. It will affect the way they play."

"If you think Den's not already planning for that, then you don't know her at all," Meg said. "Wickham tried to have a coach suspended for unsportsmanlike conduct because he didn't shake his hand after a match. He gets off on this stuff. Let's just see what tomorrow brings."

Lindsay drew in a breath and let it out slowly.

Meg stepped away, grabbing Lindsay's hand. "Come on. Don't you have a coaching session to plan for tomorrow?"

Lindsay let Meg lead her back inside, but she couldn't quiet Wickham's voice in her head. *Sham. Mockery. Washed-up.* She clenched her jaw. Maybe he was right. Or maybe, for once, she might prove him wrong.

THIRTY-THREE

Lindsay woke the next morning to a message from Den: *Check your emails.*

Her stomach tightened as she opened her inbox. The subject line glared back at her — 'Disciplinary Hearing'. She clicked it open, her skin prickling as she read. She was to front the board at 10am to answer to a charge of 'bringing the club into disrepute'.

She dragged a hand over her face and immediately thought of Wickham. Of course it would be him. He'd found a new way to get at her. Not with cheap shots and insults, but something more powerful. He was using the Old Boys' club to break her down this time.

She padded into the kitchen where Meg was making breakfast.

"Morning, did you want—" Meg stopped short when she saw Lindsay's face. "What's wrong?"

Lindsay dropped heavily onto a stool at the bench. "I've been summoned by the board."

Meg frowned. "When?"

"This morning."

Meg snatched up her phone. "I don't remember anything about a board meeting." She thumbed her phone. "I've got nothing. Show me the email."

Lindsay slid her phone across the bench and watched as Meg's face turned from confusion to anger. She handed the phone back, her eyes blazing. "I need to make some calls."

She drained the last of her coffee, set the mug in the sink and strode down the hall.

"Where are you going?"

Meg's voice filtered from the bedroom. "To fix it."

"I don't think you can," Lindsay called to her.

Meg appeared back in the hallway, pulling on her shoes. She grabbed her keys and jacket. "I can, and I will." She paused in the doorway and turned back, her expression softening. "Because it's my job."

Lindsay stood up and walked over to the coffee machine. She grabbed an extra large mug from the cabinet. She was going to need it this morning.

The boardroom smelled of bad coffee and cheap cologne. Lindsay sat on one side of the polished black table, her hands tucked into her lap. She picked at her nails, wanting the meeting to be over with. Den sat beside her, her face as neutral as Den could manage, but Lindsay could feel the heat of anger radiating off of her.

Den had been called in on a charge of insubordination. Lindsay guessed it was about yesterday's game when she played Ellie over Grace.

Across from them, two men in ill-fitting grey suits shuffled papers and avoided eye contact. The others were late. A fact that told Lindsay all she needed to know about their respect, or lack of it, for herself and for Den, and the process they were about to go through.

The door finally opened. Three men walked in. Lindsay didn't know the first one, but the other two made the blood sink to her feet. Gary. And Wickham.

Den's voice was cool and even. "What are they doing here?"

The black-haired board member cleared his throat. "We're entitled to call witnesses. And for disciplinary hearings, we can request an external observer from the Ethics Committee." He inclined his head toward Wickham.

Lindsay's stomach turned. She already had a fair idea how this hearing was going to go, and she didn't like it one bit.

"Okay, shall we start?" the black-haired man said. He introduced himself as Richard, the Chairman of the Board, and the other two board members present were Jack and Ron.

Lindsay didn't care about their names. All three of them looked overstuffed and stale. Gary sat at the end, smirking, and Wickham sat to one side, away from the table, his nose in the air, the picture of arrogance.

"Firstly, I'd just like to thank Mr Wickham for bringing this information to our attention and protecting the reputation and professionalism of the club," Richard said, shuffling his papers. "As to the reason for us being here today, Coach Denise Baker, you've been charged with insubordination. You were instructed by the board to play Grace Palmer as starting goalkeeper. Instead you fielded Ellie Fraser."

Den opened her mouth to speak but Richard raised his hand. "You'll have your turn." He glanced at his notes again and then looked up over his glasses at Lindsay. "Lindsay McAllister, you were contracted as a rookie player. You have been observed to be assuming coaching responsibilities which is outside your remit."

Lindsay's chest tightened. "That's not—"

"Ms McAllister," Jack cut her off. "We have evidence that the contract you signed was in fact fraudulent."

"No but—"

"Ms McAllister, please," Richard said.

Lindsay slumped back in her chair, her arms crossed. She could feel Wickham's eyes boring into her, but she wouldn't give him the dignity of looking back at him. It was clear she wasn't going to get a fair hearing. And neither was Den.

"We've reviewed the evidence of both charges," Richard continued.

Den leaned forward on the table, her hands curling into fists. "Evidence? You mean Gary's whining?"

Gary leaned back in his chair, his smirk widening. He said nothing. He didn't have to. The board was doing his dirty work for him.

"The Board feels that the team has lost its professionalism of late. There's been a clear lack of authority from the coaching staff." Richard checked his notes. "Am I correct to state that there was illegal gambling taking place at the pre-tournament training camp with players left completely unsupervised?"

"Correct," Gary jumped in before Den or Lindsay could reply. "The team was completely out of control. Phones out during drills, card games half the night. It was chaos."

Den shot him a look that should have killed him on the spot. "They were playing for Tim Tams, Gary. It wasn't an underground casino."

The corners of Jack's mouth twitched up but his smile was gone in a flash.

"We take gambling extremely seriously," Ron said with a nod that was almost comical.

"It's about discipline," Gary added. "A strong program starts with strong leadership."

All three board members nodded like bobble-heads. Wickham didn't move. He just sat in his corner, his eyes locked on Lindsay, barely containing his smirk.

Richard tapped his papers. "Exactly, and due to the obvious lack of leadership by current coaching staff, the decision of the board is as follows: effective immediately, Ms McAllister's contract is terminated. Coach Denise Baker, you are stood down pending a review. The club requires clear authority and professionalism, which is why we're appointing Gary—"

The boardroom door banged open.

"Sorry I'm late," Meg said, her voice casual, like she'd been invited all along and really was just running late. "Traffic was terrible." She placed folders in front of the board members, coloured tags sticking out the side. Lindsay smiled to herself.

Following in after her were three of the owners Lindsay had seen at the clinic in Toowoomba.

"What is the meaning of this!" Richard demanded.

Meg sat down beside Lindsay, the owners taking the remaining seats around the table like they owned the place. Which, Lindsay thought, they actually did. Meg gave Lindsay's leg a quick squeeze and then flipped her folder open.

"You remember Victoria, Amelia and Sally," Meg said, indicating to the owners. "I know you gentlemen are busy, so we won't hold you up. If you'd like to open your folders, you'll see I've included a copy of the purchase contract, signed by the three new shareholders," she indicated to the owners, "and signed off by the board just a few weeks ago."

The board members left their folders untouched, their faces blank, but Meg plowed on. "I'll bring your attention to clause seven point three, 'Breach of Fiduciary Duty and Reputational Harm'. It states 'Should the Board of Directors, either through action or inaction…'" She waved a hand. "Well, I don't think I need to read it all to you. Suffice it to say, this clause gives the owners a right to dissolve the board if it believes reputational harm has been caused to the club, league, or to the owners themselves."

Lindsay looked on in awe at Meg in full Ops Manager mode, silencing the suits across from her, steamrolling the meeting without even raising her voice. It was a bit of a turn on.

The board members shifted uneasily. Richard tugged at his collar. Jack shuffled his papers. Even Gary's smirk wavered.

"We're actually protecting the, er, reputation of the club," Richard stammered. "There's been a clear breach—"

"Yes, we know," Victoria cut in. Her voice was low and steady, almost like she was talking to a child. "That's why we're here." She glanced at Meg, who pulled out a single page from her folder.

Richard sputtered. "But—"

Meg put up her hand to silence him. "Mr Wickham's public accusations, which you are now using as grounds for this hearing, was a direct result of your refusal to properly manage a problematic staff member. Attempting to scapegoat Coach Baker and Ms McAllister constitutes a clear case of inflicting reputational harm."

Meg slid the paper across the table. "As this Special Resolution shows," Meg continued. "As of nine am this morning, this board has been dissolved by shareholder resolution."

The board members looked at the paper as if it was a live grenade. Which it kind of was, Lindsay mused. She glanced at Wickham. His expression finally cracked. The corner of his mouth twitched, and his air of arrogance and certainty was replaced with doubt.

"To that end," Meg said, taking the shareholder resolution and tucking it back into her folder. "This meeting is over."

The men sat for a moment, too stunned to move. Then Richard stood, tugged down his jacket, gathered his paperwork and walked out. The others followed him in a silent procession. Gary hesitated, as if he wanted to say something, but he set his lips in a stiff line and slunk out behind them. Wickham was last, his expression stormy. As he reached the door he turned.

"This won't stand." His voice was gravelly, meant to intimidate. It would have worked on Lindsay, once. Not anymore.

When the door closed, Lindsay let out a breath.

Before she could celebrate, though, Meg said, "The owners have some things to discuss before you get back to work." She gave Lindsay a smile and squeezed her shoulder. Then she left Lindsay and Den with their new bosses.

"We won't take up too much of your time," Victoria said. "Meg has filled us in."

"We know you've got a match to prepare for, and you need some certainty in your staffing," Sally added. "So as of right now, Ms McAllister— Lindsay— your rookie contract is terminated."

Lindsay's heart lurched.

"It will be replaced by a coaching contract, back-dated until the start of the pre-tournament camp," Sally said, her smile softening. "I hope that's agreeable."

For a moment, Lindsay could only blink. Then she nodded. "Yes. Yes, absolutely." She glanced at Den, who was grinning.

"And Denise," Amelia said. "You can rest assured that we won't meddle in on-field operations or team selections."

Den inclined her head. "Thank you."

Victoria rubbed her hands together. "Right. I think that's everything. We should all be getting back to work."

They stood and shook hands, the owners wishing Den and Lindsay good luck for the next game. Then the door closed behind them, leaving the boardroom suddenly quiet.

Lindsay sank into a chair. "What the hell just happened?"

Den chuckled. "You got promoted. And you heard the boss. We've got work to do."

THIRTY-FOUR

THE NEXT THREE DAYS were a whirlwind of recovery sessions, video analysis and training runs, building towards their second game against the Riverside Rovers. They were at the same divisional level as the Mustangs, receiving a wildcard entry into the tournament, and the team that Den was hoping could get them their first win.

The boardroom drama and Wickham's threat still lingered in Lindsay's mind, but she had no time to dwell on it. With her rookie contract replaced by a coaching one, the pressure felt different now. She wasn't pretending anymore. This was real.

The compact draw of the tournament meant there was very little downtime between the first few games, so while Meg was working in the office, Lindsay was out on the field with Ellie and Grace, or in one of the training rooms with Den and the other coaches watching footage and talking tactics.

Ellie and Grace were progressing well, improving every session, and Lindsay was particularly happy with Ellie's ability to bounce back from the first-game loss.

She put both goalkeepers through their paces in a set of drills focused on communication and distribution. From the footage Lindsay had seen of Riverside, her tactics for Ellie would be to play high in her box, so communication was going to be key.

Riverside relied on the speed of their forwards, and mostly played balls through the opposition back line, hoping to catch out the off-side trap. Ellie had the speed and the skills to shut those raids down, so they trained like Lindsay wanted them to play.

By the time the second match rolled around, Lindsay was confident in Ellie's ability to do a job for the team.

The second home game wasn't as well-attended as the first. Midweek games were always a tough draw, but there were still crowds of people lined up to go in when Lindsay arrived. She smiled at Ellie and Grace as she walked past on her way to the Player's Entrance. They were signing autographs, and Lindsay was taking in the atmosphere, trying to keep her adrenaline in check.

As she reached the entrance, she saw a familiar figure standing near the tunnel, deep in conversation, laughing, with a man in an official's jacket. Wickham. When he saw Lindsay approaching, he stopped talking abruptly, gave the official a pat on the shoulder and gave Lindsay a tight smirk as she walked past.

Inside the change room, Lindsay let Ellie and Grace go through their pre-match rituals. They knew the game tactics. There was no need for Lindsay to overwhelm them now. After the team completed their warm-up on the pitch, they filed back into the change room for the final pep talk.

"We run them ragged," Den said simply. "We're fitter than they are. Let's keep the ball moving. Make them chase."

As one, the team filed out and headed into the tunnel. Lindsay waited a moment, taking in the quiet of the now-empty change room to settle her nerves. By the time she reached her spot on the bench next to Den, the knot in her stomach had started to loosen.

The whistle blew, and she switched into coach mode, watching the play, making mental notes of anything she may need to adjust in Ellie's game at half-time.

As Den predicted, the Mustangs were much more evenly matched to Riverside, with the game played end-to-end for much of the first half. There were a few attempted break-aways from Riverside, but Ellie playing high in the box shut them down and quickly turned defence into attack to keep Riverside running. Just like Lindsay wanted.

She tracked the Riverside centre back. She carried the ball forward too far before passing wide, leaving a gap exposed behind her. Lindsay leaned across and spoke to Den, who nodded. During a break in play, it was relayed to their strikers.

Just before the half-time break, they got their chance. The Mustangs midfield pounced on a loose pass. Jordan darted toward the space behind the centre back. The pass from the midfield was pinpoint, splitting the defenders. Jordan, unmarked and unseen, ran onto it, the open goal in front of her.

She took a touch, looked up, and set herself for the shot. She drew her leg back, and just as she had the shot, the centre back thundered in from behind. Jordan's legs buckled and she sprawled on the turf, the ball dribbling out in front of her.

The referee's whistle sounded, awarding a free kick.

Den leapt out of her seat. "Ref! That's a card!"

The fourth official stepped over. "Calm down, coach."

"Don't tell me to calm down," Den fired back. "She's just taken our striker out."

The Mustangs physio ran onto the field to assess Jordan, who pushed herself back to her feet and waved him away. The shot from the free kick went over the bar, and moments later, the whistle went for half-time.

The team went into the change room ecstatic and energised, chattering and laughing. Even Ellie seemed relaxed. This was a good sign.

Den was part-way through her half-time talk when the door of the change room banged open. The room fell silent, as an official called Den over. Den nodded at Lindsay. "Coach Lindsay's going to finish up. I'll be back in a minute."

All eyes fell on Lindsay, and she reiterated the game plan and the importance of the counterattacks that were building from the back.

"We've had them on the back foot a few times when Ellie's gotten the ball out quickly," she said. "We need to be tracking back in the midfield to build that counter and catch them napping."

Den still hadn't returned when it was time to go back on the pitch for the second half. Lindsay let all the players file out of the room before she walked back into the tunnel. She turned to see Den arguing with officials further up. She went to investigate.

"What's going on?" Lindsay asked.

"You can't go back on the bench," the official said, trying to guide Den away.

"I'm the coach. I have to be on the bench," Den argued.

"I can't let you go back out there," the official insisted.

"I just— let me go," Den said, shrugging away from the official. "You have to take the team, Linds."

"What? Why?"

"I've been pulled from the bench," Den said. "Someone's made a complaint, and the match official has removed me from the bench."

"Who would even do that?" Lindsay asked, but as the words left her mouth, she knew exactly who it would be.

"It doesn't matter," Den said. "You have to take the team."

"But I can't," Lindsay protested.

"You have to go," the official said.

"Yes, just give me a minute," Den protested. "Yes, you can, Linds. You know the tactics, and you know the game. You'll be fine."

The official guided Den away.

"Where are you going?" Lindsay called after her.

"To sort it out. Captain's Oath," Den called back.

Lindsay trudged back up the tunnel to the entrance. She could hear the crowd echoing off the concrete. A face appeared around the corner. Wickham. He smirked, and leaned in just close enough for only her to hear.

"Coaching's not in your blood, McAllister. You'll choke, and they'll all see it."

Her chest tightened but she forced herself to lift her chin. "You've been saying that since I was seventeen. I'm still here, aren't I?"

Wickham's smirk grew wider, his voice menacing. "Exactly. Still hanging around the edges, never quite good enough to belong. Never first pick."

He skulked away, leaving Lindsay in the tunnel unable to breathe. She braced a hand against the wall, willing herself to take in air. How could Wickham still affect her the way he did?

"Linds."

She snapped her head up. Meg was standing a few metres away, her eyes wide and sharp with concern. She closed the distance, slipped her hand into Lindsay's and tugged.

"Come with me."

And before Lindsay could argue, she let herself be pulled away.

Meg bundled Lindsay back into the change room and closed the door. Lindsay dropped into a chair, sucking in air.

"What's going on?" Meg asked, her voice even but tinged with concern.

"I can't—" Lindsay's words got stuck in her throat. She felt Meg's hand on her back.

"Breathe, Linds. In through your nose, out through your mouth."

Lindsay did as she was told until finally, she felt like she was back in control. She stood up and paced and then turned. Meg stepped away, giving Lindsay some space.

"Something happened," Lindsay said through gasps of air. "Den can't coach."

"Why not?"

Lindsay shook her head. "I don't… I don't know."

Meg was silent for a moment, thinking. "Who's coaching?"

"Me," Lindsay said.

Meg didn't say anything at first. Finally she said, her voice calm, "You can do this, Linds."

Lindsay shook her head. "I can't coach this team. Wickham's right. I was never good enough."

Meg held up her hand. "Wickham doesn't know the first thing about you." She took a step forward. "He hasn't seen the impact you've had on this team. He hasn't seen the work you've put in since Den brought you on board. He thinks he knew you then, Lindsay, but he doesn't know you now."

She sucked in a breath and let it out again. She lowered her voice. "Because of you, there are two goalkeepers who feel like they can do anything."

Lindsay's eyes grew wider and she tried not to smile. Meg was always so measured and precise. So diplomatic and steady. And here she was delivering another motivational speech for the ages.

"And you know what? I know this goes right back to the first time you ran onto the field as a pro player and the shit that John Wickham put you through. I get that. I do. But this is not that time. This is so far removed from that time that it was in another life-time. Everything you've done since then has brought you to this moment.

So you need to go out there and put your money where your mouth is, McAllister. Because Ellie needs you on her side, and the team needs you in the coach's box. And do I need to remind you about the Captain's Oath? This, right now, is where you answer the call."

Lindsay rubbed at the back of her neck, her throat tight. She hated how much Meg's words made sense, and hated even more that part of her wanted to believe them. But wanting and believing were two very different things.

"You know, this putting yourself down, and not thinking you deserve the opportunities you're getting has to stop. I love you, Linds, but so help me God, if you don't go out there and show this team and this club that you can coach, and prove to Wickham, and yourself, that you belong here, I will not forgive you."

Lindsay couldn't help herself. She grinned. Meg loved her. Every other word of Meg's speech faded into the background.

Meg's face turned to confusion. "What?"

"You love me?" Lindsay asked.

Meg's mouth dropped open and then closed like a goldfish. "I… do?"

Lindsay shrugged. "You said it. Just now. 'I love you, Linds, but so help me blah blah blah'."

Meg's eyes widened and a red tinge crept up her neck and onto her cheeks. She covered her face with her hands. "I can't believe I said that. It's too soon, isn't it?"

Lindsay swept Meg up in a hug. "No, it's not," she murmured into Meg's hair. "I love you, too."

Meg pulled away and eyeballed Lindsay. "Really?"

"Of course," Lindsay replied.

Meg buried her head into Lindsay's shoulder.

"You're getting really good at these motivational speeches, by the way," Lindsay teased.

Meg slapped Lindsay's back playfully. "Shut up."

Lindsay laughed. "You're right, though. I know you're right."

Meg pulled away and looked into Lindsay's eyes. "I'm always right," she said, lifting her chin so their lips were millimetres apart. Lindsay closed the gap, and kissed her.

When they pulled apart, Meg pushed Lindsay away so she could look into her eyes. "You can't dwell on the past, Linds. This is your chance to right that wrong."

There was a knock on the door and it cracked open. It was Mike. "Refs are out."

Lindsay puffed out a breath and squared her shoulders. After a speech like that, how could Lindsay not go out there and coach?

Lindsay lingered at the mouth of the tunnel, the roar of the crowd bouncing off the concrete walls, the stadium lights spilling onto the green pitch ahead.

"You've got this, Linds."

Lindsay smiled without turning. Den had slipped in beside her.

"You okay?" Lindsay asked.

Den gave a quick nod. "Nothing I can't handle. I just have to watch the second half from the stands. Nosebleed seats, best view in the house, right?"

Lindsay snorted. "That's what they say."

Den clapped her on the back and headed up into the stands.

The fourth official said, "You good, coach?"

Lindsay drew in a breath, held it for a moment, and let it out. "Yep, all good."

She strode out of the tunnel, glancing behind the dugout. She spotted Meg in the first row. She smiled and mouthed 'You've got this'.

Lindsay swallowed hard and took her place in the dugout. Mike clapped her on the shoulder as he took his seat. "All right, Coach?"

Lindsay nodded and clapped her hands together. "Let's go," she whispered to herself. Then, loud enough for the team to hear, "Let's go!"

THIRTY-FIVE

The second half was end-to-end, Riverside and the Mustangs evenly matched, going toe-to-toe. Both goalkeepers made spectacular saves, but Ellie stayed high, shutting down Riverside raids before they could do any damage.

Late in the match, during a break in play when a Riverside player was treated for an injury, the Mustangs players crowded onto the sideline, taking in water and instructions. With the score locked at nil-all, Lindsay knew it was going to take something special to get them over the line.

"We're going to three at the back," she said. "Remi, you're going to push up into a defensive mid and Fi, you'll move into an extra attacking midfield role."

Fi blinked at her. "Coach?"

"Yes?"

"I'm normally defensive mid," Fi said.

"I know. Now you're attacking."

Fi's face twisted. "But, I don't really know how to play that."

"You've been playing high already. Do exactly what you've been doing, just higher up on the pitch. And now? Instead of clearing the ball, look to shoot."

Fi hesitated, then gave a small nod. "Okay."

The referee called for play to restart and Lindsay called their captain, Jordan over. "Fi's been running behind you all night. If they keep shutting you down, drag them in, then look for her. Get her the ball in space."

Jordan nodded and jogged back into position.

Play resumed, and Lindsay's heart kicked up. It was a gamble, and the old Wickham voice echoed in her mind. *You'll choke and they'll all see it.* She clenched her fists, silencing it. She wouldn't let him win this time.

The Mustangs continued to press high, pushing Riverside back. Then, with time running out, Ellie came out early, grabbing a ball on the edge of the box. She barked out orders, her arms moving like a traffic controller, spreading the midfield, forcing space to open up.

The ball moved down the wing, to the line, and then back inside. Lindsay tracked every touch. Fi was there, exactly where she told her to be, running behind Jordan, unmarked.

Jordan had two players hanging off her. She made her run, calling for the ball.

The midfielder threaded it through the Riverside back line. Jordan took it, back to goal. Lindsay leaned forward.

"Look at Fi," Lindsay whispered. "Come on, look at Fi."

As if she could hear her from the side line, Jordan laid it back. Fi stepped into the space, took a touch, and another, and then took her shot.

Time slowed. The ball flew, arching high. The keeper leapt, arms stretched, but she never had a chance. The ball slammed into the back of the net.

The stadium erupted. Fi froze for a second, then screamed and flung her arms wide. Jordan lifted her clean off her feet. The team swarmed them, jumping and celebrating.

Mike grabbed Lindsay by the shoulders, laughing. Lindsay grinned, and glanced up. Den was in the stands, fists pumping. Just behind the dugout, Meg was on her feet, clapping and cheering. Her eyes locked on Lindsay's, and she tilted her head and gave a little nod.

She caught Wickham's stoney gaze and she smiled to herself. His opinion didn't matter anymore.

In that moment, Lindsay finally felt it. What it was like to belong in this world again. As the Mustangs jogged back into position, Lindsay took her place on the edge of the pitch, her head high, her heart full, finally where she was meant to be.

ACKNOWLEDGEMENTS

This book came together faster than most, which meant my small team of early readers had to push me hard to get it right.

To Al, thank you for being the kind of coach every writer needs. Your constructive criticism always finds the weak spots, but you never let me forget the strengths in my stories when I can't see them myself.

To KJ, thank you for flying through that first read and then chasing me down for more "pings" of chemistry. You made sure Lindsay and Meg's relationship felt real on the page, and I'm so grateful for that.

To both of you: thank you for your unwavering friendship. It means the world to be able to call you mates.

To every player and coach I've had the privilege of playing alongside—or against—over many seasons of amateur football (soccer!). The joy, family, and grit I found along the way is what makes sport, and women's sport in particular, so unique.

To every reader who picks up one of my books and gives it a shot, thank you! As long as you want to read them, I'll keep writing them.

And finally to my wife, who is constantly asking when the next book is coming, I hope this one tides you over for a bit ;)

SR

x

ABOUT THE AUTHOR

S. R. SILCOX GREW up as a child of the 1980s and a teen of the 1990s. She played cricket in the summer and soccer in the winter, all the while with a cap glued firmly to her head. She loves team sports and barracks for the underdog.

Her favourite form of cricket is the Test Match, but she loves the smash and crash of the WBBL and BBL T20s. (*Go Brisbane Heat!*)

Her favourite authors include Malinda Lo, Erin Gough, Nicole Melleby and Will Kostakis.

She loves hearing from her readers and answers every email she gets herself. You can get in contact with her at mail@srsilcox.com.

She's also on Facebook and Instagram (just search for @srsilcox) but posts sporadically.

9 780645 850345